알바생 자르기

〈K-픽션〉 시리즈는 한국문학의 젊은 상상력입니다. 최근 발표된 가장 우수하고 흥미로운 작품을 엄선하여 출간하는 〈K-픽션〉은 한국문학의 생생한 현장을 국내외 독자들과 실시간으로 공유하고자 기획되었습니다. 〈바이링궐 에디션 한국 대표 소설〉 시리즈를 통해 검증된 탁월한 번역진이 참여하여 원작의 재미와 품격을 최대한 살린 〈K-픽션〉 시리즈는 매 계절마다 새로운 작품을 선보입니다.

The <K-Fiction> Series represents the brightest of young imaginative voices in contemporary Korean fiction. This series consists of a wide range of outstanding contemporary Korean short stories that the editorial board of ASIA carefully selects each season. These stories are then translated by professional Korean literature translators, all of whom take special care to faithfully convey the pieces' original tones and grace. We hope that, each and every season, these exceptional young Korean voices will delight and challenge all of you, our treasured readers both here and abroad.

Fiction Series

알바생 자르기
Fired

장강명 | 테레사 김 옮김
Written by Chang Kang-myoung
Translated by Teresa Kim

ASIA
PUBLISHERS

Contents

알바생 자르기
Fired

사장이 여자아이에게 처음 관심을 보인 것은 태국 바이어들을 접대한 회식 때였다.

 태국인 바이어는 미스터 쏨싹과 미스터 싹다우 두 사람이었다. 저녁에 뭘 먹고 싶으냐고 묻자 두 태국인은 수줍어하며 삼-첩-쌀, 이라고 대답했다. 그 대답을 재미있어한 이사가 저녁에 태국인들과 삼겹살을 먹을 거라고 사장에게 말했다. 그러자 사장도 그 사실을 재미있어하며 다른 약속이 없는 직원들을 불렀다. 신임 사장은 틈만 나면 회식 자리를 만들며 직원들과 스킨십을 하려 했다. 그렇게 태국인 바이어 환송회가 커져서 회사 전체 회식이 되었다. 그래 봤자 서울 사무실에 상주

The president of the company first started taking an interest in the girl while entertaining the buyers from Thailand.

The two buyers from Thailand were Mr. Ssoms-sak and Mr. Ssaktau. When asked what they'd like to have for dinner, they shyly replied, "Sam-k'yŏp-ssal." The director was amused by this response and told the president he was going to take the Thailanders for *samkyŏpsal* at night. The president was also amused and invited any employees who were free to join them.

At every opportunity, the newly appointed presi-dent called for company dinners and tried to get "touchy-feely" with the employees. Just like that,

하는 직원은 10여 명 정도이긴 했다.

이사가 데려간 고깃집에서 미스터 쏨싹과 미스터 싹다우는 다소 당황해했다. 삼겹살집은 보다 허름하고 시끌벅적한 곳인 줄 알았다고 했다. 은영은 태국인들이 어떻게 한국의 삼겹살을 잘 아는지 궁금해져서 이유를 물었다. 그러자 태국인들은 드라마 〈호텔킹〉 〈아이리스 2〉 〈미스 리플리〉 〈에덴의 동쪽〉 〈헬로 애기씨〉 〈왕꽃 선녀님〉 〈낭랑 18세〉를 보았다고 대답했다. 한국인들은 눈을 둥그렇게 떴다.

—뭔 우리는 들어 보지도 못한 드라마를 태국 사람이 보고 있어?

—이 친구들 잘 모셔야 돼. 우리가 한류를 꺼뜨리면 안 돼.

사장이 말했다.

사장은 미스터 쏨싹과 싹다우에게 '코리안 밤 샷'을 가르쳤다. 소폭을 몇 잔 마시자 다들 기분이 좋아졌다. 은영은 태국인들의 본명이 쏨싹과 싹다우 뒤로 깍따따따 으랏차차 빡까까야 깐따뻬야 하는 식으로 길게 이어지며, 그들이 탤런트 이다해의 열렬한 팬이라는 사실을 알게 되었다.

the farewell dinner for the Thailand buyers had become a company dinner with the entire staff. But "entire staff" only amounted to the ten or so employees at the Seoul office.

Mr. Ssomssak and Mr. Ssaktau were surprised by the Korean barbeque place to which the director took them. They explained that they'd expected Korean *samkyŏpsal* eateries to be shabbier and noisier. Ŭn-yŏng became curious and asked the Thailanders how they knew about *samkyŏpsal*. The Thailanders replied that they'd seen the Korean dramas "Hotel King," "Iris 2," "Miss Ripley," "East of Eden," "Hello! Miss," "Lotus Flower Fairy," and "Sweet 18." All the Koreans became wide-eyed.

"How are they watching all these dramas when we've never even heard of them?"

The president replied, "Make sure to take good care of them. We can't kill the Korean Wave."

The president taught Mr. Ssomssak and Mr. Ssaktau the Korean "Soju Bomb." Everyone felt good after a few glasses of *soju* shots dropped in beer. Ŭn-yŏng learned that their names, Ssomssak and Ssaktau, were shortened forms of longer names, which sounded like kkakttattatta, Ŭrach'ach'a, ppakkakaya, and kkanttappiya, in addition to Ssomssak and Ssaktau. She then found out that

―이 친구가, 미스 혜미를 좋아해요! 딸꾹! 이다해 닮 았다면서!

싹다우가 쏨싹의 팔을 붙잡고 말했다. 쏨싹은 얼굴이 빨개져서 부끄러워했으나 잠시 뒤에 정신을 차리고 물 었다.

―미스 혜미는 왜 회식에 안 왔나요?

―혜미 씨는 파트타이머예요.

은영이 대답했다.

―파트타이머는 컴퍼니 디너에는 못 오나요?

―그게 아니라…… 혜미 씨는 집이 멀어요. 그래서 저녁에는 다른 사람들과 잘 어울리지 않고 집에 곧장 가요.

은영의 말에 싹다우가 고개를 끄덕였다.

―쏨싹이 말을 붙이고 싶어 했는데 미스 혜미가 너무 차갑게 보여서 그러지 못했어요.

싹다우가 일러바쳤다.

―우리도 혜미 씨한테는 말 잘 못 붙여요.

엔지니어가 고개를 저었다. 자리에 앉아 있던 사람들 이 모두 웃음을 터뜨렸다.

they were big fans of the Korean actress Lee Da-hae.

Ssaktau grabbed Ssomssak's arm and blurted out, "He likes Miss Hye-mi! *Hiccup!* He says she looks like Lee Da-hae!"

Ssomssak's face flushed red with embarrassment, but he quickly recovered and asked, "Why didn't Miss Hye-mi come to the dinner?"

Ŭn-yŏng replied, "Hye-mi is only a temporary worker."

"Are temporary workers not invited to company dinners?"

"No...it's not that. Hye-mi lives far away. So she doesn't mingle with the other employees after work but goes home straight away."

Ssaktau nodded and blabbed out, "Ssomssak wanted to talk with Miss Hye-mi, but she looked so cold that he couldn't."

"It's not easy for us to talk to Hye-mi either."

The engineer shook his head. Everyone around the table laughed.

The director practically jumped out into the street and grabbed a deluxe taxi for the Thailand-ers.

이사가 차도에 뛰어들다시피 해서 태국인들에게 모범택시를 잡아 주었다.

—아이 러브 유, 코리아! 아이 러브 유 오올!

쏨싹과 싹다우가 택시를 타기 전에 외쳤다. 노래 주점에서 잔뜩 흥이 오른 한국인 직원들은 한 사람도 빠지지 않고 모두 3차 장소인 이자카야에 갔다.

—태국 애들 보기에도 그 아가씨가 쌀쌀해 보였나 보네.

사장은 오뎅탕과 마른오징어를 주문했다.

—성혜미 씨요?

은영이 물었다.

—그 아가씨는 하는 일이 정확히 뭐야? 박 차장이 뽑은 거야?

박 차장은 지금은 그만둔 은영의 상사였다.

—박 차장님이 출산휴가 들어갈 때 빈자리를 메우려고 뽑은 아가씨예요. 우리 회사 오기 전에는 무슨 중학교에서 서무를 했다던데요.

—어째 교직원 같은 분위기더라. 맨날 뚱한 표정으로 앉아 있는 게. 박 차장은 지금 그만둔 거지? 육아휴직 상태가 아닌 거지?

사장이 서울에 올라온 지는 이제 겨우 한 달이었다.

Before getting in the taxi, Ssomssak and Ssaktau yelled out, "I love you, Korea! I love you all!"

Excited from drinking at a music bar, all the Korean employees went for round three at an *izakaya*.

"I guess the girl looked cold even to the Thailanders."

The president ordered fish cake soup and dried squid.

"Hye-mi?" Ŭn-yŏng asked.

"What exactly does that girl do? Did Assistant Director Park hire her?"

Assistant Director Park was Ŭn-yŏng's direct superior, who'd quit now.

"Assistant Director Park hired her to fill her position before she went on maternity leave. I heard she worked in the General Affairs Department at some middle school before working here."

"I thought she had the feel of a school staff member or something, always just sitting there with a sulky expression. Assistant Director Park quit, right? She's not still on maternity leave, is she?"

Just over a month had passed since the president had come up to Seoul. Before that, he had been in charge of sales in P'ohang and Ulsan. The foreign president had returned to the headquarters in Ger-

그 전까지는 포항과 울산을 오가며 영업을 담당했다. 외국인 사장이 독일 본사로 돌아가고, 한국인으로는 처음으로 사장이 된 케이스다. 막 자기 업무 파악이 끝났고, 다른 사람들의 업무에 대해 알아보는 중이다. 이 순간까지 사무보조에 대해서는 신경 쓸 겨를도 없었을 것이다.

—그만두셨어요. 사장님이 서울 올라오기 며칠 전에.

박 차장이 육아휴직을 마치자마자 사표를 쓴 데 대해서는 은영도 괘씸하다고 생각했지만 그런 이야기를 남자들 앞에서 하고 싶지는 않았다.

—박 차장이 하던 일을 지금 그 아가씨가 하는 거야? 그 아가씨가 그런 걸 할 능력이 되나? 박 차장은 원래 하던 일이 정확히 뭐였지?

—원래 박 차장님이 하던 일은 총무였어요. 이것저것 잡다한 것들 다요. 회계랑 세무처리도 하셨고.

—그런데? 지금은 그걸 그 아가씨가 해?

—혜미 씨가 하는 일은 원래 박 차장님이 하던 일의 3분의 1쯤 될 거예요. 독일에서 브로슈어 오는 것들 정리하고, 울산이나 포항으로 부품 보내고, 청소 아주머니들한테 청소할 곳 알려 주고, 그런 것들이요. 우리 교육

many, and it was the first time they'd installed a Korean as president. He'd just finished settling into his new responsibilities and was now inquiring about what the other employees did. Up until now, he probably hadn't had a chance to concern himself with the office assistants.

"She quit. A few days before you came to Seoul."

Ŭn-yŏng thought it outrageous that Assistant Director Park had given her letter of resignation right after returning from her maternity leave, but she didn't want to say anything in front of the men.

"So now the girl is doing what Assistant Director Park used to do? Is she qualified for the position? What exactly did Assistant Director Park do?"

"Assistant Director Park was manager of general affairs. All the miscellaneous tasks. She also did the accounting and took care of the taxes."

"And the girl does all of that now?"

"Hye-mi does about one-third of what Assistant Director Park used to do. She organizes the brochures that come from Germany, ships parts to Ulsan or P'ohang, tells the cleaning ladies where to clean, that type of stuff. She also binds our training manuals and keeps the drinks and coffee capsules stocked."

"Then who does the remaining two-thirds?"

교재들 제본하고, 음료수랑 커피 캡슐 같은 것도 채워 놓고요.

—그러면 나머지 3분의 2는 누가 하지?

테이블 반대쪽에서 누가 재미있는 농담을 했는지 폭소가 터졌다. 은영은 괜히 사장 옆자리에 앉았다며 후회했다.

—3분의 1은 제가 합니다. 독일에서 이런저런 문의가 오면 제가 답장하고, 회계나 세금 관련 일도 제가 넘겨받았어요.

—최 과장은 원래 하던 일이 뭐였지?

—영업지원요. 사장님 포항 계실 때 저랑 일 많이 하셨잖아요!

—맞다, 맞다.

사장이 자기 이마를 때렸다.

—그러니까 박 차장이 원래 하던 일의 3분의 1은 그 아가씨가 하고, 또 다른 3분의 1은 최 과장이 넘겨받았고, 그러면 나머지 3분의 1은 누가 해?

—나머지 3분의 1은…… 음…… 그냥 없어졌어요. 원래 박 차장님이 닐스 사장님 개인 비서 역할을 하셨거든요. 통역도 하고, 레지던스 호텔도 잡아 주고, 아기

At the opposite end of the table, someone must' ve told a funny joke, since a roar of laughter burst out. Ŭn-yŏng regretted sitting next to the president.

"I do one-third. I respond to whatever inquiries comes from Germany, and I also took over the accounting and tax duties."

"And what did you do originally?"

"Sales support. We worked together a lot when you were in P'ohang!"

"Right, right."

The president tapped his forehead.

"So the girl does one-third of the work that Assistant Director Park used to do, and you took over another third. Then what about the remaining one-third?"

"The remaining one-third...well...it just disappeared. Assistant Director Park was the personal secretary to President Niels. She interpreted for him, booked his residence hotel, and registered his kids in school. Now none of that is necessary. And some responsibilities we just divided up amongst ourselves. Before, when the engineers went on business trips, the company used to book their flights and hotels. Assistant Director Park used to do all of that. But now the people going on a busi-

들 학교 등록도 해줬어요. 그런 건 이제 더 할 필요가 없게 됐죠. 또 어떤 일들은 다 조금씩 나눠 하게 됐고요. 전에는 엔지니어들 출장 갈 때 비행기 표나 호텔 예약을 다 회사에서 해줬잖아요. 그게 원래 박 차장님이 하셨던 건데, 지금은 출장 가는 사람들이 각자 예약하고 영수증도 직접 시스템에 입력하는 식으로 바뀌었어요.

─해외 출장 그거 얼마나 귀찮은지 과장님은 모르시죠? 저희가 출장을 가면 다 공장을 가는 거예요. 공항에 내려서 한참 가요. 도시하고는 완전 반대 방향. 잠도 다 공장 안에 있는 숙소에서 자요. 그런데 여자들은 맨날 화장품 사 달라, 뭐 사 달라, 왜 너만 외국 가냐……

갑자기 엔지니어가 끼어들었다.

─이 대리님, 지금 그 얘기 하는 거 아니거든요?

─그럼 무슨 얘기 하는 건데요?

─성혜미 씨 이야기 하고 있었어요.

─제가 지금 혜미 씨 얘기를 하려던 참이었다니까요. 저희가 메뚜기처럼 남의 공장만 다니다가 우리 회사에는 가끔 들어오잖아요. 그런 날에는, 딸꾹! 오늘은 남의 회사가 아니라 우리 회사다, 이런 반가운 느낌이 있는데! 성혜미 씨 제일 처음 봤을 때 제가 사무실을 잘못

ness trip make all the bookings themselves and in-put the receipts directly into the system.

"You don't know how tiresome foreign business trips are, do you? When we go on business trips, we only go to the factories. It's a long drive from the airport. In the opposite direction of the city. We sleep in dorm rooms at the factories. But girls always ask us to buy them make-up or this and that, and complain why only we get to go abroad...," an engineer suddenly butted in.

Ŭn-yŏng said, "That's not what we were discussing, sir."

"Then what were you discussing?"

"We were talking about Hye-mi."

The engineer responded: "Exactly. I was just getting to Hye-mi as well. You know how we sometimes drop in at the office after jumping from factory to factory like grasshoppers? Well, on those days, *hiccup!* we're happy since it's our office and not some stranger's factory. When I first saw Hye-mi, I thought I'd come to the wrong office since there was this stranger sitting at the front desk who didn't even look up at me."

"So she has a sulky expression. But why is she late for work so often? Her desk is often empty in the mornings," this time the director butted in.

들어온 줄 알았어요. 모르는 사람이 문 앞에 앉아서는, 저한테 눈길을 주지도 않아서.

—뚱한 표정인 건 그렇다 쳐도, 지각은 왜 그렇게 자주 하는 거야? 아침에 자리가 자주 비어 있더라.

이사도 끼어들었다.

—요즘 지하철 1호선이 고장이 자주 나서 그렇대요. 혜미 씨가 인천에서 1호선 타고 오거든요.

—나도 도봉구에서 출근해요. 지하철이 고장 나는 거야 고장 나는 거고, 회사는 제시간에 와야지. 그리고 그게 진짜 지하철 고장 때문인 거 맞아?

—보면 뭐 일을 하는 거 같지도 않아요. 뚱한 얼굴로 맨날 무슨 뮤지컬 사이트랑 일본 여행 사이트 같은 거 찾아보고 있어. 점심때도 맨날 혼자 나가서 밥 먹고. 커피점에 혼자 앉아서 책 읽고 그러는 거 내가 자주 봤어요.

엔지니어가 말했다. (유심히들 봤네. 걔가 진짜 이다해 닮았나?) 은영은 생각했다.

—그 아가씨 그거 안 되겠네. 잘라! 자르고 다른 사람 뽑아!

사장의 말에 다 같이 웃었다. (자기한테 그럴 힘이 있다는 사실을 과시하고 싶은가 봐.) 그날은 거기까지였다.

Ŭn-yŏng answered, "She says it's because the subway line 1 breaks down a lot these days. Hye-mi comes to work on line 1 from Inch'ŏn."

"I come to work from Dobong-gu. Okay, so the subway breaks down a lot. You still need to get to work on time. And are you sure that's really the reason?" retorted the director.

"It doesn't even look like she does any work. With that sulky expression, she's always surfing the Internet for musicals or Japan tours. She always goes out to eat lunch alone, and I've often seen her sitting alone in a coffee shop reading a book," the engineer butted in again.

(Well, you all kept a good eye on her. Does she really look like Lee Da-hae?) Ŭn-yŏng thought to herself.

"That girl has got to go. Fire her! Fire her and hire someone else!"

Everybody laughed at the president's words, guessing that he just wanted to show off his authority.

And with that, the night ended.

On the following Monday, all the events of Friday had been practically forgotten. But after receiving a text message from the girl, everything that was said at the dinner came back to Ŭn-yŏng.

다음 주 월요일에는 금요일에 있었던 일들을 거의 잊은 상태였다. 그랬다가 여자아이의 문자메시지 덕분에 회식 때 나눴던 이야기가 다시 생각났다.

거의 다 왔는데 좀 늦을 거 같아요, 지하철이 중간에 멈췄어요. 죄송합니다.

15분가량 지각한 여자아이는 은영을 향해 고개를 한 번 숙이고 자리에 가서 앉았다.

그날은 오전에 일이 많아서 화장실을 갈 틈조차 없었다. 은영이 떠안게 된 회계 업무는 분량 자체는 대단치 않았지만 일들이 월말에 몰린다는 점이 문제였다. 고개를 들어 건너편을 봤더니 여자아이가 무료한 표정으로 마우스 버튼을 까딱까딱 누르는 모습이 보였다. (또 뮤지컬과 일본 여행 정보 검색하나? 이번 마감을 하고 나서 천천히 회계 일을 좀 가르쳐 볼까?)

은영은 속으로 고개를 저었다. 회계 담당자는 독일 본사의 매니저와 메일을 주고받아야 한다. 비용처리에 대해서 본사 매니저가 궁금해하는 사항들이 많았다. 특히 각종 접대비에 대해서. 여자아이의 영어 실력이 그런 문의 메일에 답할 수준은 아니다. (점심은 대충 때워야겠다. 혜미에게 밥 먹고 들어올 때 샌드위치나 사다 달라고 부탁해

I'm almost there but I think I'm going to be a bit late. The subway train suddenly stopped on the tracks. Sorry.

The girl came about fifteen minutes late, nodded once in the direction of Ŭn-yŏng, and sat down at her desk.

It was so busy that morning that there wasn't even time to go to the washroom. There wasn't a lot to do for the accounting tasks Ŭn-yŏng had taken over, but it all had to be done at the end of the month. Ŭn-yŏng raised her head and looked across the room to see the girl looking bored, click-clicking the mouse. (Is she looking up musicals or Japan tours again? After I finish this month's, should I slowly start training her in accounting?)

Inwardly, Ŭn-yŏng shook her head. The person in charge of accounting had to exchange e-mails with the head office in Germany. There were a lot of details regarding the handling of expenses that the manager at the main office was curious about— especially regarding the various entertainment expenses. The girl's English wasn't good enough to respond to the inquiries. (I'll have to grab something quickly for lunch. I'll ask Hye-mi to pick me up a sandwich as she comes back from lunch.)

Just then, the girl walked towards Ŭn-yŏng.

"Would it be alright if I went to lunch and came

야지.)

그때 여자아이가 걸어왔다.

—과장님, 저 밥 먹고 병원에 갔다가 조금 늦게 들어
와도 될까요?

미묘하게 어긋난 타이밍이었다. 사무실에는 은영과
여자아이뿐이었다. 다른 직원들은 막 엘리베이터를 타
고 내려갔다. 이제 은영은 굶어야 했다.

—왜요, 어디 아파요, 혜미 씨? (그런 말을 하려거든 좀 미
리 하란 말이야. 그리고 무슨 이유로 병원에 가는지, 몇 시까지 들
어올 예정인지도 제발 좀 같이 말해줘.)

—제가 옛날에 버스에서 내리다 오토바이에 치인 적
이 있거든요. 그 뒤로 계속 다리가 저려서……. 그런데
이 근처에 좋은 한의원이 있다고 해서 다녀 보려고요.

—그래요. 다녀와요. (한의원?) 몇 시까지 올 수 있을
것 같아요?

—거기가 버스로 한 정거장이거든요. 늦어도 두 시 반
까지 올게요. 괜찮을까요?

—그래요. 다녀와요.

—돌아올 때 소견서를 한 부 받아 올까요? 그냥 이렇
게 갔다 오면 제 맘이…….

back a little late, ma'am? I need to go to the hospital."

The timing was off by a split second. There was only Ŭn-yŏng and the girl left in the office. The other employees had just gotten on the elevator. Now Ŭn-yŏng would have to skip lunch.

"Why? Are you sick?" (Why can't you ask these things a bit earlier? And also include why you need to go to the hospital and what time you think you'll be back?)

"A while ago, I was hit by a motorcycle as I was getting off the bus. Since then, my leg is always stiff and sore. I heard there was a good oriental medicine clinic around here, so thought I'd give it a try."

"Okay. (Oriental medicine clinic?) What time do you think you'll be back?"

"It's one bus stop away. I'll be back no later than 2:30. Is that okay?"

"Sure, okay."

"Should I bring back a doctor's note? I wouldn't feel comfortable if I didn't."

Ŭn-yŏng smirked. (Of course you need to submit a doctor's note. Are you kidding?)

"Did the girl go somewhere?"

The president was hovering near the girl's desk,

은영은 헛웃음을 지었다. (아니, 소견서는 당연히 제출해야지. 이 아가씨가 지금.)

—이 아가씨 어디 갔나?

사장이 여자아이의 자리 앞에서 어슬렁거리다 은영에게 와서 물었다. 여자아이가 한의원을 다니기 시작한지 보름 남짓 되었을 때였다.

—지금 병원 갔는데요. 뭐 시키실 일 있으세요? 급한거면 저 주세요.

사장은 묘한 표정을 짓더니 여자아이에 대해 이것저것을 물었다. 다니는 병원이 어디인지, 언제부터 다녔는지, 왜 다니는지. 급기야는 혜미가 병원에서 받아온 소견서까지 달라고 했다. (뭐야, 사무보조 아르바이트생 병원 보내는 것도 내 마음대로 못 하나?)

하지만 사장의 표정이 딱딱했던 것은 은영의 짐작과는 전혀 다른 이유 때문이었다. 사장은 휴대폰을 꺼내 소견서에 적힌 번호로 전화를 걸었다. 그러고는 병원에 언제 문을 열고 닫는지, 점심시간은 언제인지를 물었다.

—퇴근하고 나서도 갈 수 있는 병원이면 이 아가씨 혼을 내 주려 그랬는데.

then came and asked Ŭn-yŏng. It had been a little more than two weeks since the girl had started going to the oriental medicine clinic.

"She went to the clinic. Do you need something done? I can do it if it's urgent."

A strange look came over the president's face and he started to ask questions about the girl. Where was the clinic? When did she start going there? Why? And eventually he asked to see the doctor's note. (What—don't I even have the authority to send a part-time office assistant to the clinic?)

But the reason behind the president's stern expression was completely different from what Ŭn-yŏng had assumed. The president took out his cell phone and called the number on the doctor's note. He asked what their opening hours were, and when their lunch break was.

"I was going to say something to her if the clinic stayed open until after she finished work."

The president chewed over his words. Ŭn-yŏng was surprised that he'd check up on something as trivial as this.

"Does the girl work later on the days she goes to the clinic?"

"To be honest, Hye-mi's working hours are a bit of a problem. But no, I don't make her stay longer.

사장이 입맛을 다셨다. 은영은 사장이 그런 사소한 일까지 확인한다는 사실에 조금 놀랐다.

—이 아가씨는 이렇게 병원 갔다 온 날에는 퇴근을 늦게 하나?

—사실 혜미 씨 근태가 좀 문제이긴 한데요, 그렇다고 제가 퇴근을 늦게 시키진 않고 있습니다. 혜미 씨 일 자체가 많지 않거든요. 일도 없는데 굳이 사무실에 남길 이유는 없잖아요. 벌주는 것도 아니고.

—그 아가씨가 하는 일, 몰아서 하면 하루에 네 시간만 해도 충분한 거 아냐?

—그렇긴 합니다.

—그러면 저 아가씨한테 연봉을 60퍼센트 줄 테니 오전 근무만 열심히 하고 가라면 어떨까? 우리는 인건비 절감해서 좋고, 저 아가씨도 그 시간에 뭐 다른 걸 준비할 수 있으니 좋지 않겠어? 공무원시험 같은 거.

—예에…….

—아니면 그냥 자르자. 최 과장이 이 아가씨 하는 일 다 넘겨받고 그만큼 연봉을 올려 받으면 어때? 한 2,000만 원이면 돼?

—사장님, 혜미 씨 연봉이 2,000만 원이 안 돼요. 그

She doesn't have a lot of work to do so there's no reason to keep her here. It's not like it's a punishment or anything."

"The work she does. If she did it all at once, couldn't she finish it in four hours or so?"

"True."

"Then what if we asked her to just work in the mornings and give her sixty percent of her salary? Wouldn't it be better since we'd cut down on payroll costs, and she could have more time to look into other things? The civil service exam or something."

"Uh...sure."

"Or let's just fire her. What about you take over her responsibilities and I'll raise your yearly salary by that much? Does an extra 20,000,000 *wŏn* sound fair?"

"Hye-mi's yearly salary doesn't come to 20,000,000 *wŏn*. That would end up costing the company more."

"Her yearly salary isn't even 20,000,000 *wŏn*?"

"She gets 1,550,000 *wŏn* a month."

"I can understand 1,500,000, but what's with the 1,550,000 *wŏn*?"

"It was 1,500,000 *wŏn* up until last year, but she was given a 50,000 *wŏn* raise this year."

건 오히려 비용이 더 드는 거예요.

　—이 아가씨 연봉이 2,000이 안 돼?

　—한 달에 155만 원 받습니다.

　—150이면 150이지 155만 원은 또 뭐야?

　—작년까지는 150이었는데 올해 5만 원 인상해 준 거예요.

　—누구 맘대로?

　—박 차장님이 닐스 사장님한테 부탁해서 그렇게 됐습니다. 5만 원 인상해봤자 1년에 60이잖아요.

　사장은 잠시 생각에 잠겼다.

　—그 아가씨가 박 차장 출산휴가 갈 때 들어왔다며. 그러면 몇 달 더 있으면 우리 회사에서 일한 지 2년 되는 거 아냐? 2년 되면 정규직으로 고용해야 하는 거 아냐?

　—알바도 그 규정 적용받나요?

　은영은 뜻밖의 질문에 허둥댔다.

　—내가 사장 달고 서울에 와서 처음 거래처 사람들 만나서 인사할 때 그중 한 명이 그러더라고. 문 앞에 있는 아가씨 자르라고. 회사에 들어온 고객들이 그 아가씨 얼굴 보고 첫인상 안 좋게 갖는다고 말이야. 그런데

"By whom?"

"Assistant Director Park made a request to President Niels. A 50,000 *wŏn* raise only adds up to 600,000 *wŏn* more per year."

The president thought for a moment.

"You said the girl was hired when Assistant Director Park went on maternity leave? Then in a couple of months, it'll be two years since she started working for us. Don't we have to hire her as a permanent employee after two years?"

"Does that regulation also apply to temporary workers?" Ŭn-yŏng became flustered by the president's unexpected question.

"When I was first appointed president of the Seoul office and was going around introducing myself to our business partners, one of them told me to fire the girl at the front desk. They said that after seeing the girl's sullen face, customers would get a bad first impression when visiting the office. And that's exactly how I felt when I first met the girl. I don't know your opinion about this, but as a person running a company, these things are important. Right now, her habitual tardiness and going to the clinic during working hours isn't causing any real damage to the company. I mean, it's not like her role here is that important. But what if the

내가 그 아가씨를 처음 봤을 때 똑같이 생각했거든. 최 과장은 어떻게 생각할지 모르겠지만 조직 운영하는 입장에서는 그런 게 중요해. 지금 그 아가씨가 상습 지각하고 근무시간 중에 병원 다니는 게, 그 자체로 회사에 큰 손해를 끼치지는 않지. 그 정도로 가치 있는 일을 하는 것도 아니니까. 하지만 이러다 다른 직원들도 우리 회사는 지각쯤은 해도 상관없구나, 나도 평소에 지병 있던 것도 근무시간 중에 통원 치료를 받아야겠다, 그렇게 생각하면 어쩌겠어?

할 말이 없어진 은영은 고개를 숙였다.

—내가 앞에서 어슬렁거리니까 최 과장은 뭐 시키실 일 있느냐고, 급한 거면 자기가 하겠다고 하잖아. 나는 여태까지 그 아가씨가 그러는 걸 본 적이 없어. 사무실에 손님이 와도 불러서 시키기 전에는 차 한 잔을 내오지를 않아. 외국인 사장들이야 한국 지사를 그냥 거쳐 가는 곳으로 여겼으니까 그런 거 신경 쓰지 않았겠지. 나는 아냐.

—이게 그 아가씨를 자르라는 얘기야? 나보고 자르라고 시킨 거야?

other employees started thinking that it was okay at this company to come to work late? Or if they all started saying they had chronic illnesses and had to go for outpatient treatment during working hours?"

Ŭn-yŏng had no response and kept her head down.

"When I start hovering, you come and ask me if I need something and say you'll do it if it's urgent. But I've never seen the girl do that. When a visitor comes to the office, she doesn't even bring refreshments unless we ask her to do so. Sure, the foreign presidents probably didn't think much of it since they considered the Seoul office as just a temporary stop. But not me."

"Is he saying we should fire her? Did he tell me to fire her?" Ŭn-yŏng asked her husband as they sat at home eating delivery chicken.

"I'm not sure. Did your boss say anything after that?"

"The girl came back right at that moment, and the president received a call from Germany, so we couldn't finish. Should I just wait until the president gives the order?"

"It's a bit ambiguous. I think the girl's job itself is ambiguous. It's common for work in general affairs,

은영은 남편에게 물었다. 그녀는 남편과 집에서 배달 치킨을 먹고 있었다.

—잘 모르겠는데? 자기네 사장은 그다음에는 아무 말 도 안 했어?

—그 아가씨가 그때 막 사무실 들어오고, 사장님도 독 일에서 전화가 와서 더 말을 못 했어. 그냥 사장님이 뭐 라고 지시할 때까지 기다리고 있어야 하는 건가?

—애매하네. 그 아가씨 하는 일 자체가 참 애매한 거 같아. 원래 총무니 홍보니 마케팅이니 하는 자리가 일 을 해도 잘 티가 안 나잖아. 그런 비슷한 관리직이 두세 사람이라도 더 있으면 끼리끼리 뭉치면서 자기들 바쁘 다, 일 많다, 그런 티를 낼 텐데.

—그렇지. 우리 회사가 제대로 된 회사가 아냐. 그냥 독일 본사의 아시아 영업점 겸 애프터서비스센터인 거 야. 그러니까 영업사원이랑 엔지니어만 필요한 거고, 장부 보고 잔일 해 주는 사람은 한 명 정도 필요한데 그 게 그 아가씨인 거고. 영업직이나 기술직들 보기에는 어딜 나가서 영업 계약을 따 오는 것도 아니고 기계를 고치고 오는 것도 아니니까 이 아가씨는 뭐 하는 사람 인가 하지. 이 아가씨가 처세를 잘하는 것도 아니고.

public relations, or marketing to be less noticeable. If there were two or three more people in similar administrative positions, then they could band together and show that they were busy or had a lot of work."

"True. But things aren't done normally at our company. It's just the Asian office-slash-service center for the main office in Germany. That's why we only need salespeople and engineers. There only needs to be one person to do the bookkeeping and take care of the small stuff, and that's the girl's job. But to the eyes of sales or technical support personnel, it's not like she goes out and lands contracts or fixes the machines, so of course they question her position. And it's not like she conducts herself well, either."

"What about you? Do people think the same way about you?"

"I'm not in administration, I'm in sales support. Everybody in sales knows exactly what I do."

"What about Assistant Director Park? You said she was manager of general affairs."

"That's the clear difference between the assistant director and the girl. The assistant director was on good terms with the German president and she communicated well with her immediate superiors

─자기는? 자기에 대해서는 사람들이 이상하게 생각
하지 않아?

─나는 관리직이 아니라 영업지원이야. 내가 뭘 하는
지는 영업직들이 잘 알아.

─박 차장한테는 어땠어? 그 사람은 총무였다며.

─그게 차장님하고 이 아가씨의 결정적인 차이점인
데, 차장님은 독일인 사장이랑 친하고 본사의 직속 상
사들하고도 의사소통이 잘됐잖아. 그러니까 잘은 모르
지만 뭔가 하는 일은 있나 보다, 다들 그렇게 생각했지.
차장님은 오히려 사내의 숨은 권력자였어.

─관리직이 잘하면 또 그렇게 되지. 어느 회사나 인사
나 재무가 제일 막강해.

─나 이 아이 어떻게 해야 돼?

─자기가 하기 나름 아닐까? 자기네 사장도 별 생각
이 없을걸. 사장 자리에서 생각할 게 얼마나 많은데 뭘
알바생 거취까지 깊이 고민하겠어. 자기가 당장 자르겠
다고 하면 그러라고 할 거고 자기가 몇 달 더 쓰겠다고
해도 그러라고 하겠지. 이제 자기도 과장이잖아. 슬슬
어떤 문제는 직접 결정을 해야 할 단계지. 내 생각에는
박 차장이라는 사람이 그런 걸 잘했어. 자기가 결정 내

in the German headquarters. So although we didn't know the specific details, everyone just assumed she did her job. If anything, the assistant director held the actual power in the office."

"That's what happens with administrative positions if you do well. In every company, human resources or the financial department hold the power."

"What should I do with the girl?"

"Depends on you. I don't think your boss really cares. Your boss probably has tons to think about already. I don't think he's stressing out over a temp worker. If you tell him you're going to fire her, he'll say okay. And if you say you'll observe her for a few more months, he'll agree to that, too. You're a section chief now. You're at the stage where you should be able to make your own decisions. In my opinion, Assistant Director Park was good at that sort of thing: making decisions and getting them approved by the president."

"You're right. She was good at that."

"Just do the same."

"What would you do if you were me?"

"I think I'd just fire her and hire someone new. It doesn't seem like she's going to change her attitude, and the situation surrounding her isn't likely

리고 사장에게 승인 받는 거.

　—맞아. 차장님이 그런 걸 잘했어.

　—자기도 그렇게 해.

　—당신이라면 내 처지에서 어떻게 하겠어?

　—그냥 자르고 다른 사람 뽑을 거 같은데. 그 아가씨
일하는 태도가 바뀔 거 같지도 않고, 주변 상황이 바뀔
거 같지도 않으니까.

　—그건 싫은데.

　—왜?

　—불쌍하잖아. 지금도 거의 소녀 가장인 거 같던데.
아휴, 박 차장님은 왜 이런 애를 뽑아서 사람을 이렇게
애를 먹인담.

　—내 생각에는 박 차장이 문제가 아니라 자기가 문제야.

　—내가 뭐.

　—그 아가씨도 처음 자기네 회사에 면접 볼 때에는
그런 태도가 아니었을걸? 성격이야 싹싹하지 않았다고
해도 최소한 근태는 나쁘지 않았을 거야. 그걸 자기가
망친 거지. 지각해도 아무 말 않고, 손님 접대를 안 해도
아무 말 않고, '불쌍한 애'라고 생각하면서 계속 아무 지
적도 안 했지? 그러니까 애가 그렇게 된 거야. 사람들이

to change either."

"I don't want to."

"Why not?"

"I feel bad for her. It seems like she's providing for her whole family. Dammit. Why did Assistant Director Park have to choose a girl like her and cause me all this trouble?"

"I don't think Assistant Director Park is the problem. The problem is you."

"What did I do?"

"The girl's attitude probably wasn't like that when she first came to your company for an interview. Even if she wasn't sociable, at the very least, her attendance was probably good. You ruined that. You didn't say anything when she showed up late, and didn't say anything when she didn't bring in refreshments for visitors. You just 'felt bad for her' and didn't reprimand her, right? That's why she became like that. Not everyone is like you and me. There are people who need someone to endlessly motivate them, correct their mistakes, and to scold them. You didn't do any of this because of your misguided sympathy."

The next day afternoon, Ŭn-yŏng called the girl into the conference room. She advised her that to

다 자기나 나 같지 않아. 어떤 사람들한테는 끊임없이 다른 사람이 동기를 부여해 주고 자세를 교정해 주고 질책을 해줘야 돼. 자기는 알량한 동정심 때문에 그걸 안 한 거지.

은영은 다음 날 오후에 회의실로 여자아이를 불렀다. '조직 생활을 하려면 붙임성이 있어야 한다'는 충고에 여자아이는 눈이 붉어졌다.

—붙임성이 있다는 게 뭐예요? 사람들이 자꾸 저보고 퉁명스럽다고 하는데 저는 정말 모르겠거든요. 손님이 오시면 저도 뭔가 내드려야 한다고는 생각해요. 그런데 저희가 제대로 된 찻잔도 없고 받침도 없잖아요. 그러면 종이컵에 받침도 없이 내주기도 민망하니까 어떻게 할지 몰라서 그냥 가만히 있었던 거예요. 제가 학교에서 일할 때에는 종이컵에 담아 가는 건 예의가 아니었거든요,

—그냥 아무거나 내와도 괜찮아요. 정 모르겠으면 사장님이나 손님한테 물어봐도 되고요. 음료수 뭐 가져올까요? 커피나 주스, 어떤 걸로 가져올까요, 그렇게. 그러면 그 사람들 대답도 뻔해요. 아무거나 가져다주세

work in the corporate culture, you needed to be a "people" person.

The girl's eyes welled up. "What does it mean to be a people person? People keep saying that I'm blunt, but I don't understand. When a visitor comes, I know I should offer them refreshments. But we don't even have proper cups or saucers. It's embarrassing to just offer them something in a paper cup, so that's why I didn't do anything. I didn't know what to do. When I worked at the school, it was disrespectful to offer something in a paper cup."

"You can just take in whatever. If you really don't know, you could ask the president or the visitor. 'What would you like to drink? Coffee or juice? Which would you prefer?' Like that. Then their reply is obvious: 'Anything is fine.' Okay?"

"Last time, I brought a canned coffee to a visitor and they asked me if I was being rude."

"It was probably a close friend of the president's just joking with you. Wasn't he laughing as he said it?"

"And it's hard to ask the president anything. He's so stern. So I feel intimidated talking to him. And a lot of the time, I can't understand what he's saying because his dialect is so thick and he talks too fast.

요, 그럴 거예요.

　─저번에는 캔 커피를 들고 갔더니 손님이 그러시던데요. 이거 너무 성의 없는 거 아니냐고.

　─그건 사장님이랑 친한 분이 농담하신 거겠죠. 웃으면서 말씀하신 거 아니에요?

　─사장님한테 뭘 여쭤 보기도 그런 게, 사장님은 너무 과묵하시잖아요. 그래서 말 걸기가 겁나요. 또 사투리도 심하고 말도 너무 빠르셔서, 사장님이 뭐라고 말씀하시면 그게 무슨 말인지 알아듣지 못할 때가 많아요. 그럴 때 다시 여쭤 보기가 무서워요.

　─우리 사장님 그렇게 과묵한 분 아니에요.

　─제가 찻잔이랑 컵받침 세트라도 하나 살 수 있었으면 이런 고민을 안 했을 텐데. 제가 그런 것도 하나 제대로 살 수가 없잖아요. 당하는 사람 입장에서는 아무래도 억울하죠.

　여자아이의 눈에서 눈물이 흘러내렸다.

　─사장님이 저를 그렇게 지켜보시는 줄 몰랐어요.

　─내가 우리 구매카드로 결재를 해줄 테니까 이따가 하나 사요. 아무튼, 사장님이 혜미 씨 붙임성 이야기를 저한테 여러 번 지적을 하셨어요. (넌 혼이 나도 이미 여러

And I'm too scared to ask him again."

"Our president isn't that stern."

"If I was able to at least buy a set of cups and saucers, then this wouldn't even be a problem. But I'm not authorized to purchase anything. This feels unfair." A tear ran down the girl's cheek. "I didn't know that the president was keeping such a close eye on me."

"I'll give you my purchasing card so you can go buy a set later. In any case, the president has talked to me on numerous occasions regarding your people skills. (You should've gotten in trouble a lot more is what I'm saying.)

"I guess you got in a lot of trouble because of me."

"Would you possibly consider working only in the mornings and getting paid 800,000 or 900,000 *wŏn* a month? If you were preparing for an exam or something, it'd be better for you."

The girl's expression suddenly changed. Ŭn-yŏng got the impression that all the tears had just been an act.

"Is that what the president said? Is that what he's suggesting?"

"Frankly speaking, the work you do doesn't require you to sit at your desk all day. And I think it'd

번 혼이 났어야 했다구.)

—과장님이 사장님한테 혼이 많이 나셨군요. 저 때문에.

—혹시 혜미 씨는 월급을 80만 원이나 90만 원 정도 받고 오전 근무만 할 생각은 없어요? 뭐 시험 같은 걸 준비하는 게 있다면 그게 훨씬 유리할 거 같은데.

그 말에 여자아이가 갑자기 표정이 바뀌었다. 은영은 상대가 여태까지 흘리던 눈물이 모두 연기였던 것 같은 인상을 받았다.

—사장님이 그래요? 사장님이 그러자고 하세요?

—사실 혜미 씨가 하는 일이 그렇게 하루 종일 앉아 있어야 할 필요는 없는 거고, 또 그러는 편이 혜미 씨가 병원 다니는 데에도 좋을 것 같고……. 하루 네 시간씩 오전만 근무하고 월 90만 원을 받으면 시간당 임금은 오히려 올라가는 셈인데.

—과장님, 저 여기 출근하는 데 한 시간 반이 걸려요. 왕복 세 시간이 드는데 지금보다 월급이 깎이면 계속 다닐 이유가 없어요. 야간대학 학자금 빚진 것도 갚아야 하고……. 병원 다니는 것도 제가 다니고 싶어서 다니는 게 아니고 아파서 그러는 건데 그걸 트집 잡으시면 안 되죠.

be easier for you to go for your treatments at the clinic. If you worked only four hours each morning and got paid 900,000 *wŏn*, then your hourly pay would actually be higher."

"It takes me an hour and a half to get to work. That's three hours round-trip. If my monthly salary is cut then there's no reason for me to continue working here. I still have outstanding student loans from my night classes. And, as for going to the clinic, I'm not going because I want to, but because I'm in pain. You can't hold that against me."

Ŭn-yŏng said she understood and sent the girl back to her desk. The girl, who'd turned ice cold at the mention of a pay cut, once again put on a sad face, returned to her desk, and large tears welled up again. The male employees noticed the girl crying, but no one dared to talk to her. Ŭn-yŏng couldn't send a crying girl on an errand so she went to the bank herself. (People only care about a girl crying if she's young and pretty. If you hadn't made so many excuses, then I would've...)

It seemed like the girl was trying to be more sociable. Like a stiff robot, she awkwardly said hello when she saw people, and when visitors came, she timidly went into the president's room carrying the

은영은 알았다고 하고 여자아이를 자리로 돌려보냈다. 임금 삭감 얘기에 냉정해졌던 여자아이는 다시 슬픈 표정을 짓고 자리에 앉아 눈물을 뚝뚝 흘렸다. 남자 직원들이 여자아이가 우는 모습을 알아차렸으나 감히 말을 걸지는 않았다. 은영은 우는 아이에게 심부름을 시킬 수가 없어 직접 은행에 다녀왔다. (여자가 운다고 사람들이 신경 써 주는 것도 젊고 예쁠 때뿐이야. 네가 그렇게 변명만 늘어놓지 않았어도 내가…….)

여자아이는 싹싹해지려고 노력하는 것 같았다. 사람들을 보면 로봇처럼 어색하게 인사하고, 손님이 오면 쭈뼛거리며 새로 산 찻잔 세트를 들고 사장실에 들어가기도 했다. 하지만 그뿐이었다. 더 부지런해지거나 더 적극적으로 일하지는 않았다. 은영에게 더 도움이 되지도 않았다.

은영의 마음이 결정적으로 돌아선 건 며칠 뒤였다. 파업 중인 A자동차 회사에서 '긴급'이라고 적힌 공문이 날아왔다. 불법파업 규탄대회를 여의도공원에서 열 예정이니 협력업체에서도 직원을 한 명씩 보내 달라는 내용이었다. 그 아가씨 하루쯤 없어도 괜찮지? 사장은 현장

new set of cups. But that was it. She wasn't more diligent or enthusiastic in her work. And she wasn't any more of a help to Ŭn-yŏng.

Ŭn-yŏng finally gave up on the girl a few days later. The management at A Motors, whose employees were currently on strike, sent an official document marked "URGENT" to the office. It stated that a rally in opposition to the illegal strike was being planned at Yeouido Park, and for each partner firm to send an employee. *We can do without the girl for a day, right?* At the mention that a proof of attendance would be issued at the site, the president told Ŭn-yŏng to send the girl.

The girl's face went pale. "I don't know where Yeouido Park is."

"You expect me to believe that you don't know where Yeouido Park is? Should I google it for you?"

"What I meant was...actually, my leg still really hurts. You saw it on the doctor's note. I need to take it easy for three weeks and monitor it. If I go to the rally, don't I have to stay standing?"

"Hasn't it been three weeks already?"

"No, not yet."

"Hye-mi, then let's do this. Just go and check it out for a bit. Then you can go to a nearby coffee

에서 참석 확인증을 발급한다는 얘기에 여자아이를 보내라고 했다.

여자아이는 얼굴이 새파랗게 질렸다.

─저 여의도공원이 어디인지 모르는데요.

─아니, 혜미 씨, 여의도공원이 어디인지 모른다는 게 말이 돼요? 내가 검색해서 찾아줄까요?

─과장님, 그게 아니고요. 사실은 제가 다리가 계속 아파서요. 저번에 소견서에도 적혀 있었잖아요. 3주일 정도 안정하면서 관찰을 해야 한다고……. 그 규탄대회 가면 계속 서 있어야 하는 거 아닌가요?

─그 소견서 받아 온 지 3주일 되지 않았어요?

─아직 안 됐는데요.

─혜미 씨, 그러면 이렇게 해요. 일단 가서 분위기 보다가 근처에 카페 같은 데 가서 쉬어요. 그럴 분위기가 아니고 정 못 있겠으면 나한테 전화를 하고.

집에 돌아온 은영은 남편에게 분통을 터뜨렸다.

─진짜 깜찍하지 않아? 여의도공원이 어디인지 모른대. 가라고 하니까 나중에는 나를 확 쩨려보더라고. 어이가 없어서……. 어떻게 사람이 그렇게 아군 적군도 구별을 못 해? 사장님이 자르라고 할 때 막아준 게 누군데.

shop and rest. If you're not able to do so, then give me a call."

Ŭn-yŏng vented her anger to her husband after she got home.

"Isn't she cheeky? She said she doesn't know where Yeouido Park is. I told her to go anyway, and she glared at me. The nerve. How can a person not be able to differentiate between friend and foe? Who's the one who saved her from the president's chopping block?"

"You sure there isn't something really wrong with her leg?"

"If it was serious, then it would've said so in the doctor's note. But it only said 'suspected ligament injury.' And that's coming from an oriental medicine clinic. If I went there and complained that my leg hurt, they'd probably write the same thing. And, if her leg was so sore, how can she ride the subway every morning for an hour and a half?"

"So what are you going to do?"

"I'm going to talk to the president tomorrow. To fire her. What do you think? About firing her and asking for a raise? Do you think the president would really give me 20,000,000 *wŏn* more?"

"Not likely. And even if he does, don't take it."

"Why not?"

—그 아가씨 진짜로 다리에 무슨 장애가 있는 선 아니야?

—장애가 있었으면 병원 소견서에 그렇게 쓰여 있었겠지. 무슨 인대 손상 의심이라고 쓰여 있었어. 그것도 한의원에서 떼어 온 소견서야. 지금 내가 그 병원 가서 다리 아프다고 징징대도 똑같은 소견서 받아 올 수 있을걸? 그리고, 그렇게 다리가 아프면 매일 아침마다 지하철은 어떻게 한 시간 반씩 타고 와?

—그래서, 어떻게 할 거야?

—내일 사장님한테 얘기하려고. 자르자고. 자기는 어떻게 생각해? 그 아가씨 자르고 내 연봉 올려 달라고 하는 건? 사장님이 진짜로 2,000만 원을 올려줄까?

—그렇게는 안 올려주지. 그리고 설사 올려준다고 해도 그러지는 마.

—왜?

—어느 회사고 간에 연봉 올려주면 반드시 그 돈값 뽑아 먹어. 자기가 지금 하는 일에 그 아가씨 일만 딱 추가될 거 같아? 안 그래. 사장님이 포항에 있을 때부터 자기한테 영업 일 시키려고 그랬었다며. 영업지원만 하면 미래가 없다고, 진짜 영업을 배워야 한다고.

"At whatever company, when they give you a raise, they always make sure to get their money's worth. Do you think they'll just add the girl's workload to the work you do now? That's not how it goes. You said the president has been trying to get you into sales ever since he was in P'ohang, saying that there was no future in sales support, that you need to learn sales."

"He did."

"Well, if you do take the raise, he'll probably turn you over to sales bit by bit. Then, before you know it, you'll be doing double the work you're doing now. And I don't think that your president would give you the 20,000,000 all at once. He'll probably suggest 5,000,000 more each year over four years, or something like that. And when it comes time to negotiate your pay, he'll bring it up again and try to reject any claims you have to a further raise. It's an overall loss all around."

"Then what should I do?"

"Tell him to hire someone new. But only to work in the mornings. That way, he'll pay less than what he paid the girl. Then ask him to pay you the difference because it'll be that much more of a burden on you since the new hire won't be there all day. Then your job will stay the same, but you'll get

—어, 맞아.

　—만약 이 일로 연봉이 올라가면 사장님이 슬슬 영업 일을 자기한테 떠넘길걸? 그러면 어느 순간에 자기는 지금 하는 일의 두 배를 하게 될 거야. 내 생각에는 자기 사장이 2,000을 한 번에 올려줄 리도 없어. 4년 동안 매년 500씩 올려 주는 걸로 하자든가, 그 비슷한 식일 거야. 그리고 그거 물고 늘어지면서 연봉 협상 때 다른 인상 요인은 반영하지 않으려고 하겠지. 여러 가지로 손해야.

　—그러면 어떻게 해?

　—새로 알바생을 뽑자고 해. 대신에 오전 근무만 하는 걸로. 그러면 그 아가씨한테 들어가던 돈도 확 줄일 수 있잖아. 그만큼을 자기 연봉에 조금 반영해 달라고 해. 아무래도 알바생이 전일 근무를 하지 않으니까 자기 부담이 늘어났다고. 그러면 일은 일대로 늘어나지 않고 돈은 조금 더 받을 수 있게 되지.

　여자아이를 해고하고 싶다는 말에 사장은 단박에 찬성했다. 은영이 오전 근무만 하는 알바생을 쓰고, 알바생에게 일을 다 맡기지 않는 대신 다음 연봉 협상 때 그

paid a bit more."

The president immediately agreed when Ŭn-
yŏng told him she wanted to fire the girl. She
would hire a part-timer to work only in the mornings, but wouldn't give them the full workload. Instead, she asked that the company keep this point
in mind when it came time to re-negotiate her salary. *Nicely played*, was the expression on the president's face.

The girl listened to the notice of termination with
her head down. *We only need you until the end of the
month. Until that time, you are free to look for other employment and go for job interviews.* The girl didn't respond. Ŭn-yŏng spoke in the nuance that all of this
was the president's doing. They couldn't hire her
for a permanent position because she'd already
worked there for two years, and that was too much
of a burden for the company.

"I think he's really focused on running everything
his own way because he's the first Korean president."

"I guess being more sociable wasn't the answer,"
the girl responded.

"Hye-mi, do you have any plans after work? If
not, then do you want to have dinner with me?"

점을 어필하겠다고 제안하자 사장은 제법인네, 하는 표정을 지었다.

여자아이는 고개를 푹 숙이고 해고 통보를 들었다. 이 달 말까지만 나와 달라, 지금부터 다른 일자리 찾고 틈틈이 면접 보러 다녀도 된다는 말에 여자아이는 뭐라 대답하지 않았다. 은영은 이 모든 것이 사장 때문이라는 뉘앙스로 설명했다. 근무기간 2년을 채워서 정규직으로 만들 수는 없으니까, 그건 우리로서도 너무 큰 부담이니까.

—아무래도 첫 한국인 사장이 되시다 보니까 이것저것 의욕이 많이 생기시나 봐요. 자기 스타일대로 회사를 운영하고 싶은…….

—결국 싹싹하게 군다고 해결될 문제는 아니었네요.

여자아이가 말했다.

—혜미 씨, 오늘 저녁에 약속 있어요? 다른 약속이 없으면 같이 밥이나 먹을래요?

—학원에 가야 해서요.

—학원? 무슨 학원?

—영어학원요. 영어가 중요한 거 같아서요.

은영과 여자아이는 다음 날 패밀리 레스토랑에 가서

"I have to go to an academy."

"Academy? What academy?"

"An English academy. I feel that English is important."

The next day, Ŭn-yŏng and the girl went to a family restaurant for dinner. The girl ordered barbeque ribs. (Why do poor girls always ask to go to family restaurants and order the barbeque ribs when you say you'll buy them dinner?) Ŭn-yŏng asked the girl about the English academy.

"It's in Jongno. The lectures start at 7 p.m. In exchange for free tuition, I do things like erasing the blackboards and cleaning up."

"Oh, so that's why you always left early."

"I also mark the students' test papers. The vocabulary tests. I like marking because I feel like I'm also studying. If I get on the right subway train at Jongno, I can go all the way to Inch'ŏn without having to transfer. And since there are a lot of seats at that hour, I can memorize the words while riding the train."

The girl also talked about the other part-time jobs she'd had: gas station, restaurant, convenience store, fast-food chain, Internet cafe, amusement park, serving staff at a hotel, and she was even hired as a fake wedding guest.

함께 저녁을 먹었다. 여자아이는 바비큐 립을 주문했다. (왜 못사는 집 아이들은 뭘 사 주겠다고 하면 꼭 패밀리 레스토랑에 가자고 해서 바비큐 립을 시키는 거지?) 은영은 여자아이에게 영어 학원에 대해 물어보았다.

—종로에 있는 학원이에요. 저녁 7시부터 강의를 듣거든요. 강의를 공짜로 듣는 대신에 칠판 지우고 청소하고 그런 일들을 해요.

—그래서 매일 저녁 그렇게 일찍 갔구나.

—수강생들 시험 친 것 채점도 해요. 단어 시험 같은 거요. 채점은 저도 공부가 되는 거 같아서 좋아요. 종로에서 인천까지는 처음에 열차를 잘 타면 중간에 안 갈아타도 되거든요. 또 그 시간에는 자리가 많아서 앉아 갈 수 있으니까……. 지하철에서 막 단어 외우면서 가요.

여자아이는 자신이 했던 다른 아르바이트 일거리에 대해서도 말했다. 주유소, 식당, 편의점, 패스트푸드점, 피시방, 놀이공원에서 일했고 호텔 홀서빙과 하객 대행도 해봤다고 했다.

—제가 어딜 가도 자꾸 안 좋은 꼴을 당하니까 사람들한테 마음을 못 열고 뚱해 있는 거 같아요.

—우리도 혜미 씨랑 더 오래 일할 수 있었으면 정말

"Wherever I go, it keeps ending badly, so I think that's why I keep my distance and can't let people in."

"We would've also enjoyed working with you longer but..." (I guess her attitude at her other jobs wasn't so great either. But I suppose I should applaud her for not selling herself at bars.) That's how companies work. To the person on the receiving end, what an organization thinks is rational is quite ruthless. I'm in the same position as you. I work for them now, but if the company says 'you're fired,' I have to pack up my things."

"Did you say 'rational'? As I was filing expense receipts, I saw that just the first round for the farewell dinner with the Thailand buyers last month came to more than my monthly salary. And the entire Seoul office staff went as well. After the president arrived, he's called for a lot of these so-called company dinners. Is this also rational?"

It was the end of the month. Ŭn-yŏng took a designer scarf she'd received as a present but never used, put it in a paper bag, and went to work. The morning was busy again because it was the end of the month. The girl was staring at her computer screen with a blank expression. (Does she have to be

좋았을 텐데…… (알바 할 때도 태도가 별로 안 좋았나 보구나. 그래도 유흥업소는 가지 않았으니 용하다고 해야 하나?) 회사라는 게 그래요. 조직에서는 합리적이라고 결정하는 게, 당하는 개인 입장에서는 참 매정하죠. 나도 혜미 씨랑 똑같은 처지예요. 이러고 일하다가 회사가 너 나가, 그러면 짐 싸야지.

—합리적이라고요…… 과장님, 지난달에 태국인 바이어들 왔을 때 환송회 한 거, 제가 영수증 정리하다 보니까 1차 밥값만 제 월급보다 더 나왔던데요. 그 환송회에 서울 사무소 직원들이 다 갔잖아요. 사장님 오신 다음에 그런 식으로 회식을 몇 번이나 하셨잖아요. 그것도 합리적인가요?

31일이 되었다. 은영은 선물 받은 뒤로 한 번도 쓰지 않은 명품 스카프를 종이가방에 넣어 회사에 들고 갔다. 월말이라 오전에는 또 바빴다. 여자아이는 멍한 표정으로 모니터를 들여다보고 있었다. (마지막 날까지 저러다 갈 건가.)

저녁에 은영은 선물, 이라며 여자아이에게 종이 가방을 내밀었다. 여자아이는 놀란 표정으로 가방을 받았다.

like that until her very last day?)

After work, Ŭn-yŏng gave the bag to the girl,
saying that it was a gift. With a look of surprise, the
girl took it.

"I thought it'd be nice if you had at least one item
like this."

"But why are you giving me this?" The girl's expression was like a child's who'd just been caught
lying by her mother.

"Because it's your last day. I brought it as a farewell gift. I hope you like it."

"My last day?"

Her act of feigning ignorance was so fake that
Ŭn-yŏng let out a laugh.

"I told you we only needed you until the end of
the month. Are you going to say you don't remember? So that's why we went to Outback for dinner
together."

"You told me you didn't need my anymore, but
didn't tell me an exact date."

"You really don't remember? I told you about
three weeks ago in the conference room."

"In the conference room, I remember you telling
me that I had to quit working here. And I remember going to Outback. But you didn't tell me exactly when I should stop coming to work. I was wait-

—혜미 씨도 이런 아이템 하나쯤은 있으면 좋을 기 같아서.

—과장님, 이걸 저한테 왜요……?

여자아이는 어머니한테 거짓말을 하다 들킨 어린애 같은 표정이었다.

—마지막 날이니까, 작별 선물로 가져왔어요. 마음에 들었으면 좋겠네.

—마지막 날이라니요?

시침을 뚝 떼는 연기가 너무 부자연스러워서 은영은 그만 웃고 말았다.

—혜미 씨, 내가 혜미 씨한테 이달 말까지만 나오고 그만 나오라고 했잖아. 그게 기억이 안 난다고 할 참이 야? 그래서 우리가 아웃백도 같이 가고 그랬잖아.

—이제 그만 나오라고 하기는 하셨지만 언제부터 그 만 나오라는 말씀은 하지 않으셨잖아요.

—혜미 씨, 정말 기억이 안 나요? 3주쯤 전에 회의실 에서 얘기했잖아요.

—회의실에서 과장님이 저더러 이제 그만둬야 한다 고 말씀하신 건 기억나죠. 그래서 아웃백 갔던 것도 기 억나고. 그런데 과장님이 언제부터 그만 나오라는 말씀

ing, wondering when you'd give me my notice of dismissal."

"Notice of dismissal?"

"When you fire someone, you have to give notice in writing. Even small neighborhood convenience stores do that. And we didn't talk about my severance pay or anything, so of course I didn't think I was being fired right away."

"Severance pay?" Flustered, Ŭn-yŏng asked. The girl kept an awkward smile throughout the whole conversation.

It was a good thing Ŭn-yŏng didn't ask why a temp worker would get severance pay. According to the regulations, even temp workers were entitled to receive severance pay. When firing an employee, a notice of dismissal in writing had to be given to employees who'd worked over fifteen hours a week for more than one year. It had to be given thirty days in advance, and a clear reason stated. In the event that a company was in violation of this, a civil complaint could be filed at the local labor relations commission. Then a summons was sent to the president.

"I'm so sorry. I should've looked into it more carefully." (She completely stabbed me in the back.) Ŭn-yŏng said.

은 안 하셨잖아요. 저는 과장님이 통보서를 언제 주실
까, 하고 기다리고 있었어요.

　—통보서?

　—해고를 할 때에는 서면으로 예고를 해주셔야죠, 과
장님. 동네 편의점에서도 그렇게 해요. 그리고 퇴직금
얘기 같은 것도 전혀 안 했는데, 저는 당연히 당장 그만
두는 건 아니구나 생각했죠.

　—퇴직금?

　은영은 어안이 벙벙해져서 되물었다. 여자아이는 여
전히 어색한 미소를 짓고 있었다.

　알바가 무슨 퇴직금이냐, 라고 묻지 않아서 다행이었
다. 법규를 찾아보니 아르바이트생에게도 퇴직금을 지
급하게 돼 있었다. 1주일에 15시간 이상, 1년 이상 일한
피고용인이라면, 해고는 반드시 서면으로 통보해야 했
다. 명확한 이유를 명시해서, 30일 전에. 회사가 이걸
어기면 지방노동위원회에 민원을 접수하면 된다. 그러
면 사장에게 출두장이 날아간다.

　—죄송합니다, 사장님. 제가 미리 잘 알아보질 못해
서……

　(뒤통수를 제대로 맞았습니다.) 은영이 말했다.

"Just think of it as a good lesson learned. Hey, I just found out from you that that's the regulation. Things have gotten a lot better in Korea, I see." The president laughed.

"I don't think we can give a notice of dismissal now. Later on, she might turn it around and argue that it was a wrongful dismissal. We're a company that has more than five employees, and the girl was a paid employee of ours for more than six months. To be safe, it's recommended that we pursue this as a suggested resignation."

"So how much is the girl asking for?"

"If it's a suggested resignation, it says we should compensate her for at least three months' salary."

"Give it to her. It's fine. I have no regrets about the money. Do you know why?"

"No."

"Because I'm not giving the money to the girl, I'm giving it to you. And because I regard you as someone who does the work she's paid for."

The girl received three months' salary in cash and submitted her letter of resignation. On paper, it said she'd work until the last day of the newly started month, but she stopped working the next day. As the president signed the approval papers, he said to tell the girl to take the money and stop

—좋은 공부 했다 생각해야지, 뭐. 나도 법이 이런 건 지금 처음 알았네. 대한민국 좋아졌다, 정말.

　사장은 웃었다.

　—해고통보서를 보내는 것도 안 될 거 같습니다. 나중에 이걸 또 어떻게 부당해고라고 우길지 모르니……. 5인 이상 사업장이고, 그 아가씨가 6개월 이상 월급 근로자로 일했기 때문에 확실히 하려면 권고사직 형태로 하는 게 좋답니다.

　—그래서 그 아가씨는 돈을 얼마를 달라는 거야?

　—권고사직이면 위로금으로 석 달 치 임금을 줘야 하는 거 아니냐, 그러고 있습니다.

　—줘, 줘. 괜찮아. 나는 그 돈은 아깝지 않아, 왠지 알아?

　—아니요.

　—그 돈이 그 아가씨가 아니라, 최 과장한테 가는 돈이라고 생각하는 거야, 나는. 그리고 최 과장은 그 돈값을 하는 사람이라고 생각하는 거고.

　여자아이는 석 달 치 임금을 현금으로 받고 사직서를 썼다. 서류상으로는 새로 시작한 달 말일까지 근무하는 걸로 되어 있었지만, 사직서를 쓴 다음 날부터 출근을

coming starting tomorrow. Ŭn-yŏng had planned on doing the same. If she saw the girl, it would only make her blood boil.

They hired a new temp worker from an online job site: a young male with a fresh face. They hired him after double-checking that he was on a leave of absence from a reputable university in Seoul, didn't live too far away, and came from a stable home. They gave him 750,000 *wŏn* a month and had him work only in the mornings. They made it clear from the beginning that the employment period was only five months.

About two months later, an e-mail came from the girl: "I noticed that while I was employed at the company, I wasn't registered for the four social insurance policies. I received a consultation from the online job site, Albamon, and they said this was illegal and that in these cases, I could sue the company for failing to report my insurance deductions. But I don't want to do that. Could the company just pay me the amount for the four insurances that they didn't report?"

"And they said not to trust the two-legged beast..." Ŭn-yŏng's face was burning.

"What did the lawyer say?" her husband asked.

하지 않았다. 그거 받고 내일부터 나오지 말라고 해. 사장은 결재 서류에 사인을 하면서 말했다. 은영도 그럴 생각이었다. 여자아이 앞에 있으면 부글부글 화가 끓어 올랐다.

구인사이트를 통해 새 아르바이트생을 뽑았다. 해맑은 인상의 청년이었다. 서울 시내 괜찮은 대학을 휴학 중이었고, 집이 멀지 않았고, 집안 형편도 나쁘지 않다는 점을 확인하고 채용했다. 월급 75만 원을 주고 오전 근무만 시켰다. 처음부터 근무 기간은 5개월이라고 못을 박아 두었다.

두 달이 지났을 때쯤 여자아이에게서 메일이 날아왔다.

과장님, 제가 회사에 다니는 동안 4대 보험에 가입이 되지 않았더라고요. 알바몬에서 상담을 받아 보니까 그게 불법이라며, 이런 경우에 보험취득신고 미이행으로 회사를 고소할 수 있다고 합니다. 그러고 싶지는 않은데요. 회사가 부담하지 않았던 4대 보험비 액수만큼을 저에게 따로 주실 수 없을까요?

―검은 머리 짐승은 거두는 거 아니라더니…….

은영은 얼굴이 벌게져 있었다.

―장 변호사님은 뭐래?

"That there's no need for her even to file a suit. She just has to make an appeal to the labor administration or labor relations or whatever. The penalties are different depending on the insurance, but there's a fine for the health insurance, and for worker's compensation or employment insurance, there's only a penalty, but no fine."

"Then everything the girl said is right?"

"Yup. Crazy, huh?"

"What are you going to do? Are you going to tell the president?"

"I don't know. What should I do? Should I tell him? The Germans are really sensitive about this type of stuff. Basically, they don't trust the Korean employees. They think that we secretly break the law and embezzle funds. And since working conditions are really important to them, they have separate supervisors for this type of stuff. That's why to them, this is huge. In order to save money, the Korean office hired a temp worker but didn't register them for the official insurance policies. And they didn't even sign an official work contract. The girl knows all this. That's why she sent the e-mail only to me."

"What did the lawyer say?" Ŭn-yŏng's husband asked.

남편이 물었다.

─고소를 할 필요도 없대. 무슨 노동청? 노동위? 거기
다 진정만 넣으면 된대. 보험에 따라서 페널티가 다 다
른데, 건강보험은 벌금이 있고, 산재보험이나 고용보험
은 벌금 없이 과태료만 있대.

─그러면 그 여자애가 하는 말이 다 맞는 거야?

─응. 황당하지?

─어떻게 할 거야? 사장님한테 말할 거야?

─몰라. 어떻게 하지? 말해야 되나? 독일 사람들은 이
런 거에 엄청 신경을 쓰거든. 걔네들은 기본적으로 한
국 직원들을 불신해. 자기들 몰래 법 어기고 횡령하고
그럴 거라고 생각해. 그리고 근로조건 그런 것도 되게
중요하게 생각해서 슈퍼바이저가 따로 있어. 그러니까
걔네들 입장에서는 이건 큰 건이지. 한국 지사가 돈 아
끼려고 파트타이머 고용해 놓고는 공적 보험에 가입을
안 시켰다, 심지어 근로 계약서도 작성을 안 했다, 이런
거는……. 그 여자애도 그걸 아는 거지. 그러니까 나한
테만 메일을 보낸 거고.

─장 변호사님은 뭐래?

남편이 물었다.

"That the best thing is to reach a settlement and pay her. But, in return, to include in the settlement that she is not to take any further legal action or bring forth any issues regarding this in the future. But the money can't come from the company because we can't leave any proof. How much do you think she'll ask for? 5,000,000? 10,000,000 *wŏn*?"

"No way. You think she'd ask for 10,000,000 *wŏn*? For this?"

"Our president's yearly salary is 300,000,000 *wŏn*. If I ask him for 10,000,000 in exchange for not reporting it to Germany, then he'll probably pay."

"Let's do this: First, give the girl a call. Then ask her how much she wants. If she asks for less than 5,000,000, then we can pay her ourselves. With a signed agreement. If she asks for more than 5,000,000, then we'll tell your president."

"Are you okay with that?"

"I'll just think of it as a loss in my stocks."

"If you think about it, all of this is because of the stupid Assistant Director Park." Ŭn-yŏng said through gritted teeth, as she picked up her cell phone, but then suddenly stopped.

"This was a girl who, apart from being able to speak a bit of English, couldn't do anything properly. There are a lot of these types of girls in for-

─그냥 돈 주고 합의를 보는 게 제일 좋은 방법이래. 대신에 합의서에, 이후에 소송을 포함해서 어떤 문제제기도 하지 않는다고 적으래. 그런데 그 돈은 회사 돈으로는 못 하지. 근거를 남기면 안 되니까. 걔가 얼마나 달라고 할까? 500? 1,000?

─설마. 뭐 이걸 갖고 1,000만 원이나 달라고 하겠어?

─우리 사장님 연봉 3억이야. 1,000 달라고, 대신 독일에 알리지 않겠다고 하면 줄걸?

─이렇게 하자. 일단 그 여자애한테 전화를 걸어. 그리고 얼마 원하는지 물어보자. 그래서 500 미만으로 달라고 하면 그냥 우리가 주자. 합의서 받고. 500 넘게 달라고 하면 그때는 사장님한테 말하고.

─그래도 괜찮아?

─주식으로 잃은 셈 치지 뭐.

─생각해 보면 이게 다 박 차장 그 인간 때문이야.

은영이 전화기를 집어 들다 말고 이를 갈았다.

─영어 좀 하는 거 말고는 제대로 하는 게 하나도 없는 여자였어. 외국계 회사에 그런 여자들 많아. 뭘 알아보지도 않고 사람을 그렇게 뽑아 놔? 그것도 그렇게 딱

eign companies. How could she hire someone like this without even doing a proper background check? And a backstabber to boot."

"You didn't know that about her either."

"Know what?"

"You took pity on her and went easy on her. You saw her as a victim because she was naïve and weak, and because she looked poor and stupid. So you looked down on her. But that's not the case. You said she'd had a string of temporary jobs. She's learned from experience and knows the tricks of how to fight and survive in that world. If you think of it the other way around, in that world, we are the weaker ones. You and me both, we've never had to scuffle with the owner of a gas station over unpaid wages."

Ŭn-yŏng's anger started to flare, but her husband was also right. She bit down on her lip and called the girl.

"What did she say?"

Ŭn-yŏng smirked. "She wants 1,500,000 *wŏn*."

The two of them went for a drink that night.

"Seriously. Humans are the scariest."

Ŭn-yŏng put down her beer glass and sighed.

The next day, the girl came to the office, got the money, and even though she'd signed the agree-

뒤통수 칠 애로?

―그건 자기도 몰랐잖아.

―뭘?

―걔 불쌍하다고, 잘 봐주려고 했었잖아. 가난하고 머리가 나빠 보이니까 착하고 약한 피해자일 거라고 생각하고 얕잡아 봤던 거지. 그런데 실제로는 그렇지 않거든. 걔도 알바를 열 몇 개나 했다며. 그 바닥에서 어떻게 싸우고 버텨야 하는지, 걔도 나름대로 경륜이 있고 요령이 있는 거지. 어떻게 보면 그런 바닥에서는 우리가 더 약자야. 자기나 나나, 월급 떼먹는 주유소 사장님이랑 멱살잡이 해본 적 없잖아?

부아가 치밀었지만 남편 말이 옳았다. 은영은 입술을 깨물고 전화를 걸었다.

―뭐래?

전화를 끊자 남편이 물었다.

은영은 헛웃음을 지었다.

―150만 원 달래.

그들은 그날 저녁 술을 마셨다.

―사람이 제일 무섭다, 정말.

맥주를 마시다 말고 은영은 한숨을 쉬었다.

ment, didn't leave.

"Do you think I could get five copies of a certificate of employment?" The girl asked.

"Certificate of employment?"

"Yes. I forgot to ask last time."

(If the company you're applying to looks at the certificate
of employment and contacts me for a reference check, then
I'll...No, forget it. There's no need for me to tell you this.
There's also a world that only I know and you don't.)

Ŭn-yŏng clamped her mouth shut and printed
out five English copies of the certificate of employment. The girl carefully examined the certificate.

"It says that I worked here as a 'staff assistant'.
Could you possibly change it to 'administrator'?
When I worked here, I was the sole person in
charge of general affairs, not an assistant to any-
one."

Ŭn-yŏng made the changes that the girl request-
ed. As the girl was leaving the office, Ŭn-yŏng finally opened her mouth: "Was this the plan all
along?"

The girl stopped. It seemed like she was at a loss
for words. She just stood there, unable to move.

"Goodbye," the girl said. Instead of giving a direct
answer, the girl stood in front of the elevator after
bowing good-bye.

다음 날 사무실에 찾아온 여자아이는 돈을 받고 합의
서에 서명한 뒤에도 바로 나가지 않았다.

　―과장님, 경력증명서 다섯 부만 받을 수 있을까요?

　여자아이가 물었다.

　―경력증명서?

　―네. 전에 까먹고 못 받아서요.

　(그 증명서를 보고 너를 경력 채용하려는 회사가 나한테 평판
조회를 부탁하면 내가…… 아니, 됐어. 그런 걸 너한테 가르쳐 줄
필요는 없지. 너는 모르고 나만 아는 세계도 있거든.)

　은영은 입을 다물고 영문 경력증명서를 다섯 부 발급
해 주었다. 여자아이는 그 증명서를 유심히 읽었다.

　―과장님, 제가 여기 스태프 어시스턴트라고 돼 있는
데요, 혹시 어드미니스트레이터로 바꿔주실 수 없나
요? 제가 여기서 혼자 총무 일을 한 거지, 누구를 어시
스트한 건 아니잖아요.

　은영은 여자아이가 원하는 대로 서류를 만들어 주었
다. 여자아이가 사무실을 나설 때 은영은 겨우 입을 열
었다.

　―이게 처음부터 다 계획이 돼 있던 거니?

　여자아이는 걸음을 멈췄다. 말문이 막힌 듯했다. 여자

While waiting for the elevator, the girl put her hand in her purse to check and make sure the envelope was there. She was scared that she might drop the envelope and lose it. (It would've been better if they'd wired the money to my account instead of giving it to me like this.) She planned on going to the bank as soon as she left the building. She was under pressure because she was late on her student loan payments. Her leg was still sore. She'd used all of her severance pay to get surgery for her ligament injury, but it didn't seem like it'd gotten any better. The elevator door closed and she was all alone.

아이는 그렇게 몇 초간 꼼짝 않고 서 있었다.

　—안녕히 계세요.

　여자아이는 대답 대신 고개를 숙이고 엘리베이터 앞에 섰다.

　엘리베이터를 기다리면서 여자아이는 가방에 손을 넣어 봉투를 확인했다. 봉투를 땅에 떨어뜨리고 돈을 잃어버리게 되지 않을까 겁이 났다.(이렇게 주지 말고 계좌로 부쳐줬으면 좋을 텐데.) 건물을 나서자마자 은행을 찾아갈 참이었다. 학자금 대출을 제때 갚지 못해 독촉을 받고 있었다. 여전히 발목이 아팠다. 인대 수술을 받느라 퇴직금을 다 썼지만 별로 나아진 게 없는 것 같았다. 엘리베이터 문이 닫혔고, 주변에는 아무도 없었다.

창작노트
Writer's Note

안녕하세요. 장강명입니다. 「알바생 자르기」는 영어로 번역된 저의 첫 소설입니다. 그런데 아마 영어권 독자들이 이 소설을 이해하기는 쉽지 않을 것 같습니다. 한국어 사용자라면 익숙한 몇 가지 상황을 제가 소설 속에서 설명하지 않고 건너뛰었기 때문입니다. 그렇게 생략한 설명을 이 글에서 풀어보고자 합니다.

● 한국 대기업과 중소기업의 관계

한국은 불과 몇십 년 만에 가난한 나라에서 선진국으로, 독재국가에서 민주국가로 발전했습니다. 그러나 이같은 변화는 아직 완전하지 않아서, 한국 사회의 겉과

Hello, I'm Chang Kang-myoung. "Fired" is my first story to be published in English. As such, I think English readers might have difficulty understanding it. This is because in the story, I skip the explanations for various situations that are common knowledge to Korean readers. Therefore, I have included these notes to try and explain the background information.

● The relationship between large businesses and small businesses

In the period of only a few decades, Korea has advanced from a poor nation into a developed one; from a dictatorship into a democracy. But since this

속은 무척 다릅니다. 급격한 발전의 부작용과 후유증도 큽니다.

무엇보다 그러한 발전의 이득을 모든 사람이 고루 보지 못하고, 일부 기업과 계층에게 수혜가 집중됐다는 점이 가장 큰 문제입니다. 그 대표적인 수혜자로는 대기업과 대기업 대주주 일가, 그리고 대기업 직원들이 꼽힙니다. 이는 한국 정부가 50년 가까이 대기업 주도의 경제발전 전략을 써 왔기 때문입니다.

이로 인해 한국 경제는 각 부문에서 대기업 의존도가 높습니다. 종종 한국 대기업들은 이런 우월한 지위를 이용해 소비자나 자신들이 거래하는 중소기업을 상대로 횡포를 부리기도 합니다. 정부기관이 개입해 이런 갈등을 해소하는 경우도 자주 생깁니다. 그래서 역설적으로 한국 대기업들은 (소비자나 거래 회사가 아닌) 국민 전체의 여론과 정부의 반응에 민감하게 반응합니다.

「알바생 자르기」에서 은영과 혜미가 일하는 회사도 대기업에 기술을 납품하는 작은 기업입니다. 이들이 거래하는 대기업 자동차회사 중 한 곳은 자기네 공장에서 파업이 일어나자 서울 도심에서 그 파업에 반대하는 시위를 열려 합니다. 국민 여론을 자기들에게 유리하게

transition is not yet complete, there is a profound discrepancy between Korean society as seen from the outside and from within. The side-effects and after-effects of this rapid development are also great.

The biggest problem is that not everyone has profited equally from this development, and the benefits have been concentrated within certain large businesses and certain classes of society. The most visible benefactors are the large businesses, shareholders and their families, and the employees of large businesses. This is because for about fifty years, the Korean government has relied on a system of economic development that is driven by these large businesses.

Because of this, the dependence on large businesses by all sectors of Korea's economy is high. Occasionally, these large businesses use their supreme status to tyrannize consumers or the small businesses they do business with. There are many cases where government agencies must intervene to resolve the conflicts. Paradoxically, large Korean businesses react sensitively to national public opinion and government reactions (not to the consumer or small businesses).

In "Fired," the company for which Ŭn-yŏng and

만들기 위해서입니다. 이 대기업은 또 자기들과 거래하는 회사에서 직원들을 한 사람씩 그 시위 장소로 보내 달라고 요청합니다. 은영의 회사에서 사장은 짜증을 내면서도 혜미를 시위 현장에 보냅니다. 대기업의 요구를 묵살하기 어렵기 때문입니다.

● 한국 사회 갈등의 새로운 핵, 세대 갈등

오늘날 한국 사회가 겪고 있는 가장 큰 갈등은 바로 세대 갈등입니다. 크게 세 세대가 정치적, 경제적으로 매우 다른 견해를 갖고 경쟁하는 중입니다.

먼저 1960년대 이전에 태어난 노년층입니다. 한국 전쟁과 가난을 체험한 이들은 정치적으로 매우 보수적이며, 경제적으로도 '대기업 주도 성장발전전략'에 호감을 품고 있습니다. 정관계나 법조계, 상류층 사회에서는 아직 이들 세대의 영향력이 큽니다.

다음으로, 1960~1970년대에 태어난 중년층입니다. 이들은 사회 각 분야의 주역을 맡고 있으며 정치적, 경제적으로 진보 성향을 보입니다. 이들은 자신들이 한국의 민주화를 이뤄냈다는 자부심이 큽니다. 그런 만큼 이후 세대들에게 위선적, 이중적이라는 비판을 거세게

Hye-mi work is a small business that provides technical support to large businesses. In the story, a factory owned by one of the large automobile companies they do business with goes on strike, and the large company plans a rally in the center of Seoul, in opposition to the strike. Their aim is to turn the nation's public opinion favorably to their side. The automobile company requests that each company they do business with send an employee to the rally. Even while complaining, Ŭn-yŏng's boss decides to send Hye-mi to the rally. Simply put, it is impossible to ignore the request made by a large business.

● A new focus point in Korea's societal conflict: conflicts between generations

The biggest source of conflict that Korean society faces today is between generations. This is because the political and economic views of the three major generations differ vastly.

The older generation is comprised of those born before 1960. Having experienced the Korean War and poverty, they are extremely conservative in their political views, and as for the economy, they look favorably upon the "system of economic development that is driven by large businesses." In

사고 있기도 합니다.

　중년층은 한국 경제의 혜택이 일부 계층으로 집중됐다는 데 분노하고 이를 강하게 비판합니다. 그러나 자신들 역시 수혜자이며, 자신들 다음 세대는 그런 혜택을 입지 못했다는 데 대해서는 침묵합니다.「알바생 자르기」에서 은영 부부와 사장이 속한 세대가 바로 이 세대입니다.「알바생 자르기」는 이 세대의 위선 의식을 풍자하는 이야기이기도 합니다.

　다음으로, 1980년대 이후에 태어난 젊은 세대가 있습니다. 혜미가 속한 세대입니다. 한국 경제가 저성장 국면에 들어간 뒤 사회에 진출한 이들의 경제적 여건은 부모 세대에 비해 매우 열악합니다. 특히 뒤에 설명할 '한국 노동시장의 양분화' 현상과 맞물려 이들 세대는 매우 불리한 처지에 서게 되었습니다.

● 한국의 노동시장은 어떻게 양분되었나

　1980년대 이전까지 한국은 극심한 노동탄압 국가였습니다. 노동자들의 권리는 거의 보호받지 못했고, 기업이 노동운동가에게 물리적인 폭력을 가하는 일도 흔했습니다. 정부는 노조 지도자를 종종 불법적으로 체포

political relations, legal circles, and upper-class society, the influence of this generation is still strong.

The next generation is the middle generation, made up of those born in the 1960s and 1970s. These are the people who play the leading roles in all sectors of society. They have progressive political and economic tendencies. They feel extreme pride in the fact that they were the ones who brought democracy to Korea. But equal to this pride, they are harshly criticized by the younger generations for being hypocritical and having a double standard.

The middle generation does feel rage at the fact that the benefits of Korea's economy are concentrated within certain classes of society, and they harshly criticize the members of these classes. However, they are also benefiters, and stay silent regarding the fact that the generation following them can't receive benefits. In "Fired," the generation that Ŭn-yŏng, her husband, and her boss belong to this middle generation. "Fired" can also be seen as a story that satirizes this generation's hypocritical attitude.

The last generation is the youngest, born after the 1980s. This is the generation that Hye-mi be-

하고 고문했습니다.

1990년대부터 최근까지, 한국 사회가 민주화되면서 노동자들의 권익도 향상되었습니다. 이러한 노동운동은 조직력이 있는 대기업과 공공부문 노조를 중심으로 진행되었는데 2000년대에 들어서는 '대기업 및 공공부문 노조 이기주의'로 변질되었다는 지적을 받고 있습니다. 한편으로는 고성장 시기에 각종 노동자 보호법이 장기적인 고려 없이 양산되어서, 오히려 노동시장을 경직시켰다는 비판도 나옵니다.

오늘날 한국의 노동시장은 거의 둘로 나뉘었다고 해도 과언이 아닙니다. 이른바 '정규직'이라고 부르는 노동자 그룹이 있습니다. 정규직은 임금이 높으며, 기업이 이들을 해고하는 것은 거의 불가능에 가깝습니다. 1990년대 이전에 대기업에 채용된 노동자들, 이후에 노동시장에 들어온 엘리트 노동자들, 그리고 공공부문 직원들은 정규직입니다. 일부 전문가들은 '정규직'이라는 명칭 대신 '영구직'이라는 용어를 도입해야 한다고 주장합니다.

각종 노동자 보호법의 허점을 피해 최근 한국 기업들이 많이 사용하는 고용 형태를 '비정규직'이라고 부릅니

longs to. Having entered into society after Korean's economy has fallen into a state of slow growth, the members of this generation face a harsher financial reality. Particularly, when joined with the "bipolarity of Korea's labor market" (which I will discuss next), the people of this generation are placed in an extremely disadvantageous position.

● The bipolarity of Korea's labor market

Before 1980, Korea was a nation under intense labor repression. There was no protection for the rights of workers, and it was common for large businesses to exercise physical abuse against labor activists. Often the government would illegally arrest union leaders and torture them.

From 1990 to the present, as Korea has become democratized, the rights of workers have also improved. This type of labor movement was centered on large businesses with organizational power and public-sector unions. However, starting in 2000, these labor movements have been criticized as degenerating into "collective egotism of large business and public sector unions." There is also criticism that since the labor protection laws were made during a period of rapid development, without any consideration of the long-term effects,

다. 몇몇 전문가들은 이들을 '임시직'이라고 부르는 게 더 옳은 표현이라고 말합니다. 이들은 정규직과 같은 일을 해도 훨씬 적은 급여를 받으며, 해고나 부당노동 행위 같은 문제에 있어서 정규직과 같은 보호를 받지 못합니다.

「알바생 자르기」에서 은영은 정규직이고, 혜미는 비정규직입니다. 최근 몇 년 사이 비정규직에 대한 보호법이 생겼는데, 많은 고용주는 그런 보호규정이 생긴 사실 자체를 잘 모르고 있습니다. 은영과 사장도 혜미로부터 여러 가지 비정규직 보호규정에 대해 듣고 어리둥절해 합니다.

● 서울 위성도시 주민의 삶과 지하철 1호선

「알바생 자르기」에서 혜미가 사는 곳은 서울의 위성도시 중 하나인 인천입니다. 인천은 원래는 서울의 위성도시가 아닌, 역사가 깊은 도시입니다. 그러나 서울의 영향력이 점점 커지면서 '서울 경제권'에 편입되었습니다.

서울의 인구는 약 1,000만 명이며, 서울 외곽 인구는 1,000만 명보다 많습니다. 서울의 위성도시 주민들 상

they actually stiffened the labor market.

Today, it isn't an exaggeration to say that Korea's labor market is split into two groups. The first is "regular workers." They receive a high salary, and it is nearly impossible for companies to fire them. Regular workers include workers who were employed by large businesses before the 1990s, workers of the elite class who entered the labor market after 1990, and public-sector workers. Several experts argue that the term "permanent employee" should be introduced to replace the title "regular worker."

Currently, the form of employment that many companies opt for in order to take advantage of the loopholes in the labor protection laws is non-regular employment. Some experts say that it is more correct to call it "temporary" employment. These temporary workers do the same work as regular workers, yet receive lower pay and do not receive protection regarding issues of dismissal or unfair labor practices.

In "Fired," Ŭn-yŏng is a regular worker and Hye-mi a temporary worker. In the past few years, laws have been created to protect temporary workers, but many employers are unaware of the existence of these protective regulations. Ŭn-yŏng and the

당수는 서울의 직장으로 출퇴근합니다. 비싼 땅값을 감당하지 못해 서울 외곽에 집을 구한 사람들입니다. 이 중에는 출퇴근에만 매일 3시간 이상을 들이는 사람도 드물지 않습니다. 위성도시 거주자들의 주요 출퇴근 수단은 지하철입니다. 서울의 지하철 노선은 대부분 서울 바깥으로, 위성도시들로 이어집니다.

서울과 인천을 잇는 지하철 1호선은 가장 먼저 생긴 지하철 노선이고, 매우 낡았습니다. 걸핏하면 고장이 나는 노선으로, 또 저소득층이 이용하는 노선으로 악명이 높습니다.

혜미는 다리를 다친 이유에 대해 "버스에서 내리다 오토바이에 치였기 때문"이라고 설명합니다. 이런 사고 역시 버스정류장과 보행로가 잘 정비된 서울보다는 인천에서 발생하기 쉬워 보입니다.

● 한국의 직장 문화와 양성평등 문제

한국의 정치제도는 어느 수준의 절차적 민주주의를 이뤘지만, 기업이나 학교의 문화는 여전히 권위주의적입니다. 한국의 많은 직장인과 학생들은 상사나 교사에게 반대 의견을 말하기 어려워합니다. 「알바생 자르기」

president are stunned when they learn from Hye-mi that there are various types of protective regulations for temporary workers.

● The lives of residents of Seoul's satellite cities, and subway line 1

In "Fired," the place where Hye-mi lives is one of Seoul's satellite cities, Inch'ŏn. Inch'ŏn wasn't originally a satellite city of Seoul, but was a city rich in its own history. But as Seoul's influence spread, it was incorporated into the economic region of Seoul.

The population of Seoul is around ten million, but the population of the outer cities of Seoul exceeds ten million. A considerable number of residents of Seoul's satellite cities work in Seoul. These are people who can't afford the expensive housing costs in Seoul, so they live in the outer cities. It is not uncommon for many of these people to commute more than three hours to work. The primary method of transportation for the residents of these satellite cities is the subway. Most of Seoul's subway lines travel outside Seoul, to the satellite cities.

Subway line 1, which runs from Seoul to Inch'ŏn, was the first subway line to be created, and therefore is extremely old. It is notorious for breaking

에서 은영이 사장의 말에 압박감을 느끼고 사장의 본심을 궁금해하는 것은 이 같은 이유 때문입니다. 허심탄회하게 사장에게 진의를 물어보고 혜미를 어떻게 처리할지 논의한다는 것은 은영에게 거의 불가능한 일입니다.

한국 사회의 민주화, 탈권위주의화는 현재도 진행 중이며, 특히 직장 내 양성평등 문제는 이제 겨우 논의가 막 시작된 단계입니다. 「알바생 자르기」에서 은영과 혜미는 모두 직장에서 여성으로서 상대적 약자의 처지에 있습니다. 은영은 제대로 책임을 다하지 않고 편하게 직장 생활을 하다가 가정으로 돌아가 버린 선임자를 못마땅하게 생각합니다. 그러면서도 그녀는 혜미의 어려움에 대해서는 별 관심이 없는 이중적인 모습을 보여줍니다.

down frequently and is considered the mode of transportation for low-incomers.

Hye-mi explains her leg injury as: "I was hit by a motorcycle as I was getting off the bus." The probability of this type of accident occurring is also higher in Inch'ŏn than in Seoul, where the bus stops and pedestrian walkways are better maintained.

● **The issue of workplace culture and gender equality**

To a certain degree, Korea's political system has arrived at a procedural democracy; but an authoritarian culture is still present at workplaces and schools. Many employees and students find it difficult to voice their opposing opinions to their bosses or teachers. In "Fired," Ŭn-yŏng feels pressured by the president's words, and this is also the reason why she is curious about the president's true intentions. But for Ŭn-yŏng, having a candid discussion regarding the president's real intentions regarding Hye-mi's dismissal is out of the question.

Democratization and independence in Korea's culture is still ongoing, and, in particular, discussions regarding the issue of gender equality have now just started to take place. In "Fired," Ŭn-yŏng and Hye-mi are both relatively in the position of a weak subordinate within the company. Ŭn-yŏng disapproves of her previous superior, who took it easy at work and didn't act responsibly, then quit to go back to her family. But she is also two-faced in that she doesn't show much interest regarding Hye-mi's difficult situation either.

해설
Commentary

갑을의 윤리 감각

정은경 (문학평론가)

장강명의 「알바생 자르기」는 '갑을' 관계에 대한 일반
적인 편견과 기대 지평을 뒤집어버리고 묘한 지점에서
독자를 불편하게 하는 소설이다. 무슨 말인가 하면, 흥
미로운 스토리텔링이라면, 응당 〈미생〉의 장그래 같은
착하고 정의로운 비정규직 약자가 등장하여 골리앗 같
은 상사의 파렴치하고 뻔뻔한 탄압에 맞서 싸우는, 그
런 분명한 '선악 대립'의 구도가 있어야 한다는 말이다.
그런데 장강명의 「알바생 자르기」를 읽기 시작하면, 어
느 순간 알바생 '을'을 자르려는 '갑'에게 공명하고 감정
이입되어 응원하는 독자 자신의 모습을 발견하게 된다
는 것이다. 어떻게 된 일일까?

Superior and Subordinate: A Sense of Ethics

Jung Eun-kyoung (literary critic)

Author Chang Kang-myoung's "Fired" is a story
that completely overturns the common biases and
"horizons of expectation" regarding the relationship
between the "superior" and the "subordinate." This
odd focal point makes the readers feel uncomfort-
able. In other words, traditionally to be considered
interesting storytelling, a story's structure must
should be built around a clear conflict between
good and evil, such as in the Korean TV drama
"Misaeng." In this drama, the character Chang Kŭ-
rae is a good-hearted and righteous underdog
who is hired as a temporary employee and stands
up to his Goliath of a boss, who is a shameless and
brazen oppressor. But from the onset of the story,

「알바생 자르기」의 주된 초점화자는 과장 '은영'이다. 은영이 회사 측을 대변하는 '갑'이라면, '을'은 비정규직 아르바이트생 '혜미'이다. 이들이 다니는 회사는 독일에 본사를 둔 한국 지사이며 직원 10명 안팎의 소규모 조직으로 전문화, 체계적 시스템과는 거리가 먼 곳이다. '혜미'는 이곳에서 일종의 총무 및 잡일을 맡아 보고 있는 아르바이트생인데, 중요한 업무 책임자가 아닌 만큼 그게 문제 될 것도 없는 그런 소소한 존재이다. 그러나 그런 '혜미'의 '존재감'은 탤런트 이다해를 닮은 미모로 드러나고, 그런 미모에 '차갑고 뚱한' 태도로 일관한다는 데서 사람들의 이목을 끌게 된다.

태국인 바이어 환송회 겸 회식 자리에서 한국 드라마 팬인 태국인 바이어가 이다해를 닮은 '미스 혜미'를 찾자, '파트타이머라 컴퍼니 디너'에 참석하지 못한 미스 혜미의 차갑고 뚱한 태도, 작은 지각과 '보면 뭐 일하는 거 같지 않게' 뮤지컬 사이트와 일본 여행 사이트나 들여다보고 있는 일과, '점심때도 맨날 혼자 밥 먹고' 등의 행동 등이 직원들의 입에 오르내린다. 술김에 "그 아가씨 그거 안 되겠네. 잘라!"라고 말한 이후, 사장은 진지하게 미스 혜미를 정규직으로 고용해야 하는 2년이 되

the reader finds themselves resonating with, empathizing with, and cheering on the superior who wants to fire the subordinate part-timer. Why is this so?

In "Fired," the main focal narrator is Ŭn-yŏng, a section chief. With Ŭn-yŏng, representing the company, as the "superior," the "subordinate" is the temporary worker Hye-mi. The company they work for is the Korea branch for a company, headquartered in Germany; as a small organization, with around ten employees, it is a far cry from being specialized or having a structured system. Hye-mi is a temporary worker who takes care of general affairs and miscellaneous tasks. Since her duties aren't that important, her existence is minor and there is no need to focus on her. However, her presence is made known due to the fact that she resembles the Korean actress Lee Da-hae, and she continues to attract attention because of her pretty face and constantly "cold and sulky" attitude.

During a farewell dinner turned company dinner with two buyers from Thailand, one of them, who is a huge fan of Korean dramas, starts looking for "Miss Hye-mi," saying she looks like Lee Da-hae. Hye-mi is not present at the company dinner since she "is only a temporary worker," and the other

기 전에 '자르고' 싶어하는 마음을 노골적으로 드러낸다. 그러나 중간자 '은영'은 "불쌍하잖아. 지금도 거의 소녀 가장인 거 같던데."라며 혜미를 보호하려고 한다. 은영은 "조직 생활을 하려면 붙임성이 있어야 한다"는 훈계로 적당히 혜미를 교정하는 한편 자신의 '알량한 동정심'을 무마한다.

그런 은영의 마음과 달리, '혜미'는 묘한 타이밍에 은영을 불편하게 한다. 업무가 많아 점심 식사 대용으로 샌드위치라도 부탁하려 하자 혜미는 근처 한의원에 다리 치료를 받으러 가고, 급기야 불법파업 규탄대회에 가서 '참석 확인증'을 받아오라고 하자 "여의도 공원이 어디인지 모르겠는데요."라며, 다리가 아파서 못 간다고 말한다.

"진짜 깜찍하지 않아? 여의도 공원이 어디인지 모른대. 가라고 하니까 나중에는 나를 확 째려보더라고. 어이가 없어서…… . 어떻게 사람이 그렇게 아군 적군도 구별을 못 해? 사장님이 자르라고 할 때 막아 준 게 누군데." 화가 난 은영은 결국 알바생 혜미를 자르기로 결심하고 사장의 흔쾌한 승인을 얻어 혜미에게 해고를 통보한다. 그러나 '알바생 자르기'는 그렇게 쉽게 완수되

employees start commenting on her cold and sulky attitude, frequent tardiness, daily routine of "surfing the Internet for musicals and Japan tours" and not doing any work, and her "always [going] out to eat lunch alone." Having had a few drinks, the president says, "That girl has got to go. Fire her!" and afterwards he openly and earnestly expresses his desire to "fire" Miss Hye-mi before her two-year term is finished and she has to be hired as a permanent employee. But caught in the middle, Ŭn-yŏng says, "I feel bad for her. Seems like she's providing for her whole family," and tries to protect Hye-mi. By warning Hye-mi that "to work in the corporate culture, you have to be a 'people' person," Ŭn-yŏng tries correcting Hye-mi while at the same time, pacifying her own "misguided sympathy."

But contrary to Ŭn-yŏng's efforts, Hye-mi's "timing [is] off by a split second" and she makes things harder for Ŭn-yŏng. On a busy day, just as Ŭn-yŏng was about to ask Hye-mi to pick her up a sandwich for lunch, Hye-mi says she needs to go to a nearby oriental medicine clinic to get treatment for her leg. And, ultimately, when Hye-mi is told to go to a rally in opposition to an illegal strike and bring back a "proof of attendance," she re-

지 않는다. 통보한 월말이 되어 명품 스카프를 내미는 은영에게 혜미는 이렇게 반격한다. "마지막 날이라니요? (…) 회의실에서 과장님이 저더러 이제 그만둬야 한다고 말씀하신 건 기억나죠. 그래서 아웃백 갔던 것도 기억나고. 그런데 과장님이 언제부터 그만 나오라는 말씀은 안 하셨잖아요. (…) 해고를 할 때에는 서면으로 예고를 해주셔야죠, 과장님. 동네 편의점에서도 그렇게 해요. 그리고 퇴직금 얘기 같은 것도 전혀 안 했는데, 저는 당연히 당장 그만두는 건 아니구나 생각했죠."

당황한 은영은, '1주일에 15시간 이상, 1년 이상 일한 피고용인이라면, 해고는 반드시 서면으로 통보해야 한다.'는 관련 법규를 찾아내고 결국 '명확한 이유'가 불안한 은영과 사장은 권고사직 형태로 석 달 치 임금을 위로금으로 주고 해고를 마무리한다. 그러나 두 달 뒤 다시 혜미로부터 '일하는 동안 4대 보험에 가입되지 않았다, 보험취득신고 미이행으로 회사를 고소할 수 있다, 4대 보험비 액수만큼 따로 챙겨달라'는 메일을 받는다.

머리 꼭대기까지 화가 난 은영은 근로계약에 민감한 독일 본사를 거치지 않고 자비로 처리하기로 한다. 500~1,000만 원 사이를 예상했던 은영은 겨우 '150만

sponds that she "[doesn't] know where Yeouido Park is" and says she can't go because her leg hurts.

"Isn't she cheeky? She said she doesn't know where Yeouido Park is. I told her to go anyway, and she completely glared at me. The nerve. How can a person not be able to differentiate between friend and foe? Who's the one who saved her from the president's chopping block?" Enraged, Ŭn-yŏng finally decides to fire Hye-mi, and after readily receiving approval from the president, she gives Hye-mi her notice of termination.

But firing a temporary worker doesn't end that easily. On the last day of the month, Ŭn-yŏng gives Hye-mi a designer scarf as a goodbye present, but Hye-mi counters: "My last day? ...In the conference room, I remember you telling me that I had to quit working here. And I remember going to Outback. But you didn't tell me exactly when I should stop coming to work···When you fire someone, you have to give notice in writing. Even small neighborhood convenience stores do that. And we didn't talk about my severance pay or anything, so of course I didn't think I was being fired right away."

Flustered, Ŭn-yŏng looks into the regulations and sees that "a notice of dismissal in writing had to be

원'을 말하는 혜미의 요구대로 낙찰을 보고, 돈을 받으러 온 혜미는 '스태프 어시스틴트'를 '이드미니스트레이터'로 깐깐하게 교정한 경력증명서까지 챙긴다. 분에 찬 은영은 "이게 처음부터 다 계획이 돼 있던 거니?"라며 그녀를 힐난한다.

「알바생 자르기」의 핵심은 '을'을 해고하는 일이 호락호락하지 않으며, 을을 대표하는 혜미가 결코 착하고 약한 피해자가 아니라는 것이다. "걔 불쌍하다고, 잘 봐 주려고 했었잖아. 가난하고 머리가 나빠 보이니까 착하고 약한 피해자일 거라고 생각하고 얕잡아 봤던 거지. 그런데 실제로는 그렇지 않거든. 걔도 알바를 열 몇 개나 했다며. 그 바닥에서 어떻게 싸우고 버텨야 하는지, 걔도 나름대로 경륜이 있고 요령이 있는 거지. 어떻게 보면 그런 바닥에서는 우리가 더 약자야. 자기나 나나, 월급 떼먹는 주유소 사장님이랑 먹살잡이해본 적 없잖아?"라는 은영 남편의 말대로, 갑 편에 서 있는 은영이 '싸움'에서는 오히려 숙맥에 헛똑똑이고 순둥이인 피해자이고, 을인 혜미는 영악하고 뻔뻔한 강자처럼 보이는 것이다. 은영에 감정이입되는 독자는 혜미가 '을'답지 않게, '싹싹하거나 고분고분하지' 않으며 허드렛일에 분

106

given to employees who'd worked more than fifteen hours a week for over one year." Unsure if there is also a "clear reason," Ŭn-yŏng and the president resolve the situation by giving the girl three months' salary as compensation for her "suggested resignation," and then fire her. But two months later, Hye-mi sends Ŭn-yŏng an email saying, "While I was employed at the company, I wasn't registered for the four social insurance policies...I could sue the company for failing to report my insurance deductions...Could the company just pay me the amount for the four insurances?"

Completely enraged, Ŭn-yŏng decides to pay Hye-mi with her own money instead of reporting it to the main office in Germany, since they are "really sensitive" about issues regarding employee contracts. She anticipates a figure around 5,000,000 to 10,000,000 *wŏn*, but Ŭn-yŏng closes the deal with Hye-mi who suggests a mere 1,500,000 *wŏn*. When Hye-mi comes to pick up the money, she also asks for a certificate of employment, which Ŭn-yŏng agrees to and even makes the change from "staff assistant" to "administrator," as Hye-mi scrupulously requests. Outraged again, Ŭn-yŏng lashes out at the girl and asks: "Was this the plan all along?"

The bottom line of "Fired" is that it's not easy to

주하지도 않으며, 근무시간에 뮤지컬과 여행 사이트나 기웃거리고, 지각과 치료를 핑계로 불성실하며, 근로노동법을 내세워 '갑'을 몰아세울 수 있다는 사실에 분노한다. 그러나 이러한 불편한 심기는 '갑'이 느낄 수 있는 일종의 허위적 윤리 감각에 불과하다.

을인 '혜미'의 입장에서 보면, 1호선의 잦은 고장으로 지각이 불가피하고, 제대로 된 찻잔 하나 없는 회사에서 손님 접대를 하기란 옹색하기 짝이 없는 일이고, 교통사고로 인해 다친 다리를 치료하는 것 또한 어쩔 수 없는 일이다. 게다가 학자금 대출 독촉을 받고 있는 데다 퇴직금을 인대수술에 다 써버린 '혜미'에게 4대 보험 합의금 또한 그녀가 생각해낼 수 있는 가장 합법적인 생계비였던 것이다. 혜미의 지적대로, 조직의 합리성이라는 게 하루 저녁 회식비보다 못한 알바생 월급을 아까워하고 그것마저 삭감하려는 냉혹한 계산에 불과하고, 그리고 그 비용으로 '싹싹함'으로 포장된 남성들의 성적 요구까지 알은 체 해달라는 것이라면 이를 과연 정당하다고 할 수 있는가.

최근 보도에 따르면, 노동부는 2010~2014년 5년간 최저임금법을 어긴 48,349건을 적발했지만 사법처리

fire a "subordinate," and that Hye-mi, representing the "subordinate," is ultimately not a naïve and weak victim. As Ŭn-yŏng's husband explains: "You took pity on her and went easy on her. You saw her as a victim because she was naïve and weak, and because she looked poor and stupid. So you looked down on her. But that's not the case. You said she'd had a string of part-time jobs. She's learned from experience and knows the tricks of how to fight and survive in that world. If you think of it the other way around, in that world, we are the weaker ones. You and me both, we've never had to scuffle with the owner of a gas station over unpaid wages." As such, Ŭn-yŏng, on the side of the "superior," is actually the weak, naïve, and ignorant victim in this "battle," and Hye-mi, the "subordinate," is the clever, brazen, and stronger force. Readers who empathize with Ŭn-yŏng become outraged because Hye-mi doesn't act like a "subordinate." She isn't "sociable or submissive," she isn't diligent in her work, she surfs Internet sites for musicals or vacations during working hours--but she can still push the "superior" into a corner by raising the issue of labor laws. But this feeling of discomfort is merely a kind of false sense of ethics that the "superior" feels, and the ending of the sto-

를 위해 검찰에 이송된 것은 55건에 불과했다고 한다. 근로자의 편에 서야 하는 근로감독관은 노동자들의 민원에 '대한민국에서 노동법을 다 지키면 어떻게 사업을 하겠느냐'고 되려 짜증을 내는 경우가 허다하다고 한다. '을'인 혜미가 정당하게 요구하고, 악착같이 챙기는 근로법은 거의 실효성이 없을 뿐 아니라, 실제로 '을'의 방어적 무기가 되지도 못하는 것이 현실이다. '갑'인 은영이 괘씸해하고 못마땅해 하는 이들의 윤리 감각이란 을이 이 '무력한 법'을 실제로 가동시키겠다고 위협한 것일 테지만, 을의 입장에서 보면 그것은 품위나 윤리 따위와는 거리가 먼 '생존'의 문제인 것이다.

이 간극 사이에서 어떤 양태의 싸움과 반전이 일어난다 해도 패자는 언제나 '을'이다. '쉬운' 해고가 아닐 수 있겠지만 '해고'의 주체는 언제나 '갑'이고 그들이 자르는 건 '을'의 양심이나 윤리가 아니라 '생존'이기 때문이다. 「알바생 자르기」에서 장강명이 놓치지 않고 있는 부분은 바로 이것이다.

ry makes this message.

When considered from Hye-mi's perspective, there was no avoiding her being late for work since subway line 1 broke down frequently, they were poorly prepared to receive visitors and offer them refreshments since they didn't have proper cups; and the treatments for her leg were necessary since she'd been hurt in an accident. On top of that, she was under pressure because she was late on her student loan payments and she'd already used her entire severance pay for a ligament surgery. So asking the company to pay her the amount for the four insurance policy deductions was the only legitimate way she could think of to get money. As Hye-mi points out, the company spends more than a temp worker's entire monthly salary on a single company dinner and yet they begrudgingly pay her and even try to cut her wages. What an organization deems as rational is merely a heartless calculation, and if they're asking that in exchange for her wages, she's supposed to "be sociable" and acknowledge the men's sexual advances, then is it really justifiable?

According to recent reports, during 2010-14, the Ministry of Labor uncovered 48,349 cases of violations against the Minimum Wages Act, yet only 55 cases were sent to the prosecutor's office for legal action. Instead of standing behind the workers, it is said that the labor supervisor more often gets irritated and is quoted as saying, "It is impossible to run a business in Korea if you follow all the labor laws." In reality, the labor laws that Hye-mi, the subordinate, so tenaciously clings to and deems justified are practically useless and fail in their purpose as weapon to defend the subordinate. Ŭnyŏng, the superior, regards the subordinate's sense of ethics as outrageous and offensive since they threaten to actually use these ineffective laws against the superior. But from the perspective of the subordinate, it has nothing to do with dignity or ethics, but is simply an issue of survival.

Within this rift, no matter what type of conflicts or twists arises, the subordinate is always the victim. It may not be an "easy" dismissal, but the one doing the firing is always the superior, and what they are hurting isn't the subordinate's conscience or ethics, but rather, their survival. This is the underlying theme in Chang Kang-myoung's "Fired."

비평의 목소리
Critical Acclaim

기본적으로 이야기를 직조해내는 능력이 뛰어난 작가였다. 그래서 오히려 의심의 눈초리를 주게 되었는데, 이 작가가 정교한 클리셰에 능한 사람이 아닌가 하는 것이었다. 하지만 작품을 다시 읽고 난 다음 의심은 사라지고 강한 믿음이 생겼다. 이 작가, 현실을 직시하는 충실함에 둥지를 틀었다. 그 둥지 안에서 알을 깨고 부화한 것은 뭉클한 감동이다. 이 작가의 둥지 안에는 이야기를 품은 어린 새들이 더 많이 들어 있을 것 같다. 털갈이를 마치고 날아오를 준비까지 모두 끝낸 어린 새들. 이제 날아오를 일만 남았다. 앞으로 보여줄 힘찬 날갯짓이 너무나 궁금하다.

천운영, 「제20회 문학동네작가상 심사평」, 《문학동네》,

문학동네, 2015

Fundamentally, he is an author who has an exceptional ability to weave together a story. At first, this actually made me view his work with a skeptical eye. I questioned whether he was in fact proficient only in recreating an elaborate cliché. After reading the story again, though, my doubts vanished and I became a firm believer. This author has built a nest of unwavering commitment to confronting reality straight on. What cracked and hatched in this nest is a deep and moving emotion. And I believe that in this author's nest are more fledglings that hold stories within them. These fledglings have finished molting and are ready to fly. All that's left for them is to take off. I wait in anticipation to see the forthcoming fluttering of their strong wings.

Cheon Un-yeong,

"20th Munhakdongne Writer's Award - judge's commentary,"

Munhakdongne (Paju: Munhakdongne, 2015)

88만 원 세대를 대표하는 주인공의 묘사가 대단히 사실적이고 생생함에도 불구하고, 독자들은 이 소설 속에서 적지 않게 충격을 받게 될 것이며 공감과 반동 사이에서 갈등하게 될 것이다.

심사위원단, 「제16회 한겨레문학상 심사평」

논쟁적이기를 마다하지 않는 작가의 등장이 반갑다.

신형철, 「추천의 말」, 『표백』, 한겨레출판, 2011

Despite the extremely realistic and vivid portrayal of the main character as representative of the "880-thousand-won generation," readers will still be considerably shocked by the contents of the story and torn between empathy and antipathy.

Judge's committee,

"16th Hankyoreh Literature Award - judge's commentary"

It's a pleasure to meet an author who isn't afraid to be controversial.

Shin Hyung Cheol, "Testimonial,"

The Bleached (Seoul: Hankyoreh Publishing, 2011)

K-픽션 013
알바생 자르기

2015년 10월 12일 초판 1쇄 발행
2023년 09월 21일 초판 6쇄 발행

지은이 장강명 | 옮긴이 테레사 김 | 펴낸이 김재범
기획위원 정은경, 전성태, 이경재
편집 강민영, 김지연 | 관리 홍희표 | 디자인 나루기획
인쇄·제책 굿에그커뮤니케이션 | 종이 한솔PNS
펴낸곳 (주)아시아 | 출판등록 2006년 1월 27일 제406-2006-000004호
주소 경기도 파주시 회동길 445(서울 사무소: 서울특별시 동작구 서달로 161-1 3층)
전화 02.3280.5058 | 팩스 070.7611.2505 | 홈페이지 www.bookasia.org
ISBN 979-11-5662-173-7(set) | 979-11-5662-174-4(04810)
값은 뒤표지에 있습니다.

K-Fiction 013
Fired

Written by Chang Kang-myoung | **Translated by** Teresa Kim
Published by ASIA Publishers
Address 445, Hoedong-gil, Paju-si, Gyeonggi-do, Korea
(Seoul Office: 161-1, Seodal-ro, Dongjak-gu, Seoul, Korea)
Homepage Address www.bookasia.org | **Tel.** (822).3280.5058
First published in Korea by ASIA Publishers 2015
ISBN 979-11-5662-173-7(set) | 979-11-5662-174-4(04810)

바이링궐 에디션 한국 대표 소설

한국문학의 가장 중요하고 첨예한 문제의식을 가진 작가들의 대표작을 주제별로 선정!
하버드 한국학 연구원 및 세계 각국의 한국문학 전문 번역진이 참여한 번역 시리즈!
미국 하버드대학교와 컬럼비아대학교 동아시아학과, 캐나다 브리티시컬럼비아대학교 아시아
학과 등 해외 대학에서 교재로 채택!

바이링궐 에디션 한국 대표 소설 set 1

바이링궐 에디션 한국 대표 소설 set 2

Through literature, you
bilingual Edition Modern

ASIA Publishers' carefully selected

Set 1	Set 2

Division

Industrialization

Women

Liberty

Love and Love

Affairs

South and North

Set 3	Set 4

Seoul

Tradition

Avant-Garde

Diaspora

Family

Humor

Search "bilingual edition

can meet the real Korea!
Korean Literature

22 keywords to understand Korean literature

Set 5	Set 6
Relationships	Fate
Discovering	Aesthetic Priests
Everyday Life	The Naked in the
Taboo and Desire	Colony

Set 7

Colonial Intellectuals Turned "Idiots"

Traditional Korea's Lost Faces

Before and After Liberation

Korea After the Korean War

korean literature"on Amazon!

〈K-픽션〉 시리즈는 한국문학의 젊은 상상력입니다. 최근 발표된 가장 우수하고 흥미로운 작품을 엄선하여 출간하는 〈K-픽션〉은 한국문학의 생생한 현장을 국내외 독자들과 실시간으로 공유하고자 기획되었습니다. 〈바이링궐 에디션 한국 대표 소설〉 시리즈를 통해 검증된 탁월한 번역진이 참여하여 원작의 재미와 품격을 최대한 살린 〈K-픽션〉 시리즈는 매 계절마다 새로운 작품을 선보입니다.